Escape From Hehl

Issac Brooks

CONTENTS

BLOOD ON PORCELAIN

PROLOGUE

As Katie's Tesla clawed its way up the winding driveway, the gravel under its tires screamed in protest. The morning mist clung to the earth like a shroud, making the approach to the Hehl Mansion even more ominous. There it stood—a three-story Victorian monstrosity, its facade a grotesque tapestry of peeling paint and sinister ivy. Barred windows glared down, their grimy panes resembling the vacant stare of the dead.

"Jesus Christ," she muttered, killing the engine. The car fell silent, save for the rhythmic tick-tick of its cooling engine, like the calm before a storm.

Katie hadn't seen this forsaken place since she was sixteen—a naive girl trailing after Mimi, lost and clueless. Now, at thirty-two, the mansion's once grand aura had decayed into nothing more than a skeletal echo of its past splendor.

Her phone erupted with a shrill chirp, shattering the silence. She yanked it from her blazer, her lips twisting as she read her boss's blunt command:

'Don't fuck this up, Katie. The Hehl estate is worth millions. Close the deal.'

"No pressure, right?" She scoffed and tossed the phone onto the passenger seat, straightening her blazer as she caught sight of her reflection in the rearview mirror. Dark circles haunted her eyes, the silent witnesses to countless nights tormented by property listings and the relentless chase for commissions.

A rickety diesel growl tore through her thoughts as an ancient Ford pickup chugged into view. Its rusted frame groaned under the strain, a pathetic creature gasping its last. It shuddered to a halt beside her sleek Tesla, exhaling a cloud of exhaust like a dying breath.

Paul clambered out, his steel-toed boots crunching on the gravel. He slung his heavy tool belt over a shoulder, his face carved with deep lines from years of toil and sun. He cast a wary glance at the mansion.

"This the place?" He spat onto the ground, his disdain clear as day. "Looks like a goddamn death trap."

Katie stepped from her car, her practiced smile fixed in place. "Oh, come on, Paul. Where's your sense of adventure?"

"Left it back home with my common sense." He adjusted his tool belt, the jangle of his keys echoing like a death knell. "This place? Gives me the fucking creeps."

"It just needs a bit of love," Katie insisted, her heels stabbing the stone path as she led the charge to the front steps. "A lick of paint, some new wires—"

"Yeah, yeah," Paul grumbled, trudging behind her. "Just don't expect any miracles. This dump's probably got a wiring system straight out of the dark ages."

They reached the crumbling steps, each groan under their weight sounding a morbid warning. The massive oak door loomed ahead, its brass handle tarnished to near oblivion. Katie's hand shook as she reached for the key, the cold metal biting her flesh—a grim welcome to the Hehl Mansion's dark heart.

The ancient door moaned on its hinges as Katie nudged it open, a gust of stale, musty air assailing her senses and twisting her features in disgust. Dust danced in the scant sunlight that managed to pierce through the filth-coated windows, catching in the beams like minuscule ghosts of the past. Her heels tapped a morose rhythm against the warped floorboards, their echo haunting the cavernous foyer.

"Shit." She swiped at a cobweb that dared cling to her sleeve, smearing grime across the pristine navy of her blazer. "This hellhole's even more fucked up than I remembered."

Paul swept his flashlight across the expanse, the light slicing through the gloom to reveal the tragic grandeur of peeling wallpaper and a staircase spiraling into darkness like a promise of peril. His beam hesitated on an unsettling sight—the heavy-duty locks clamped on both sides of the front door, like silent sentinels.

"Who the hell cages themselves in?" His voice carried a ripple of disquiet.

"Paranoia from the previous tenants, probably." Katie's laugh echoed, a hollow sound that seemed to mock her. Brushing a dust-laden side table with her finger, she recoiled at the grim residue coating her skin. "Speaking of which..."

Paul's eyebrow arched, his flashlight's beam catching the cracked edges of a family portrait looming above the fireplace. "Previous tenants?"

"The Hehls." Katie's tone softened, a somber note threading through. "Lived here when the world went to shit in 2020—pandemic times. The whole block thought they were disease spreaders." A lump formed in her throat as she remembered Mimi's tear-streaked face. "One day, they just... vanished. Left without a word, probably couldn't handle the hate anymore."

"Just disappeared, huh?" Paul's voice was thick with skepticism.

"Well..." Katie's lips twisted into a sly grin, her fingers miming a spectral dance. "There's talk they never left. Rumor has it their corpses are moldering in the walls."

Paul's face hardened, unamused. "That's not fucking funny."

"Tough crowd," Katie murmured, her facade of levity crumbling as she returned to her professional demeanor. "Basement's that way. Circuit breaker should be somewhere down there. Get the power up, and we can start making sense of this mess."

Paul's heavy boots thudded toward the basement, his tool belt clanging with each step, his grumbles fading into the bowels of the house like the growls of a discontented beast.

Left alone, Katie couldn't shake the eerie sensation of invisible eyes upon her. The wallpaper seemed to squirm in the corner of her vision, and yet, when she dared a direct glance, it settled into an eerie stillness.

"Pull yourself together," she whispered, pulling out her notepad. She forced herself to scribble down potential renovations, each note a desperate attempt to anchor herself to reality rather than succumb to the creeping dread gnawing at her sanity.

Katie's fingers ghosted along the banister, parting the thick dust that clung to the once-polished wood—a whisper from a time when the mansion didn't seem so forlorn. Her mind drifted back to those breathless summer nights, racing up these stairs with Mimi, their laughter a vivid contrast to the empty echoes now haunting these halls.

"Girls!" The sharp rebuke from Mrs. Hehl sliced through her reminiscence, the memory so potent Katie's hand recoiled from the banister as if burned. Mrs. Hehl had mastered the art of disdain, her glares like daggers aimed straight at Katie's less-than-privileged upbringing.

After the echoes of Mrs. Hehl's footsteps had retreated, the night would soften again. Beneath blankets, she and Mimi whispered of dreams and secrets, a fragile bubble in that suffocating house. But as the months wore on, Mimi's spark dimmed, her smiles grew empty, and their conversations faltered into weighted silences.

"Should've seen the cracks," Katie muttered, wiping the dust from her palms. The isolation, the venomous whispers of the neighborhood, Mrs. Hehl's oppressive grip—it had all spiraled into a maelstrom that had swallowed Mimi whole.

An alarming creak behind her brought her back into reality. Katie whipped around, pulse racing—only shadows flickered in response. She forced a laugh through clenched teeth. "Pull it together. It's just an old house."

The thud of heavy footsteps on the basement stairs shattered the eerie calm. Paul burst through the doorway, his face ashen, his eyes wide with a terror that chilled the air. His tool belt clanged discordantly as he staggered, nearly losing his grip on his flashlight.

"Power's up," he gasped, his voice strangled with fear. "But fuck this, I'm out."

"Paul?" Katie edged closer, her voice laced with alarm. "What the hell scared you down there?"

He shook his head, his eyes darting wildly, as if expecting some horror to leap from the shadows. "No paycheck is worth this. This place—it's all kinds of wrong." His voice was a raspy whisper, terror etched into every word. "There's something down there... watching."

"Wait, what do you mean—something's watching?" But her question fell on empty air.

Paul was already fleeing, his boots thundering over the wooden porch. The front door slammed open with a violent bang, echoing through the empty house as he made his escape. His truck engine growled angrily, gravel flying as he raced away from the nightmare behind.

Frozen in the dim light of the foyer, Katie felt the weight of his words settle like a shroud. The house groaned, settling deeper into its foundations, and somewhere in the depths of the shadow-laden hallways, a door clicked shut, as if sealing away the secrets it harbored.

Katie's heels hammered a desperate rhythm across the foyer's ancient tiles as she retreated from the door, the terror from Paul's harrowing exit clinging to her like a second skin. Her heart thundered, a wild cacophony that drowned out the eerily creeping silence of the mansion, now punctuated only by the nascent hum of reawakened wires.

"Get your shit together," she hissed, hands trembling as they tried to smooth her blazer into some semblance of professionalism. But the mansion's atmosphere had thickened; the air turned viscous, heavy with unspoken threats. Dust motes, caught in the weak sunlight, spun in patterns too deliberate, too accusing.

Reaching for her phone in a bid for normalcy, her fingers froze over her boss's contact before the screen flickered and died. "Perfect, just fucking perfect," she muttered, stabbing the power button futilely. "Dead? But it was fully charged..."

A whisper sliced through the stillness, ethereal and chillingly familiar. "Katie..."

Her breath hitched, head whipping around to the empty space behind her. "Paul? This better not be your idea of a fucking joke..."

The whisper caressed her ears again, softer, more elusive. "Katie..."

Spinning, her heels screeched against the floorboards, every echo a pulse in the mansion's vast, shadow-choked heart. The air seemed to thicken, clinging to her as she faced the imposing family portrait hanging above the fireplace, its painted eyes tracking her every move with silent accusation.

A deliberate creak sounded from the dining room, pulling her breath into a sharp intake. Rational thoughts raced to attribute the noise to the house settling or old pipes—heavy denial to mask the crawling dread.

Another creak, unmistakably intentional, echoed a sinister invitation. Katie found herself drawn towards the sound, her legs betraying her terror-driven paralysis. The dining room's entrance yawned wide, shadows within stretching like dark fingers.

"Hello?" Her voice was a tremulous whisper, betraying her fear. "Is anyone there?"

Her eyes, adjusting to the murky depths, discerned a figure shrouded in shadow. It remained motionless and uncertain. A shard of sunlight, defying the grime-streaked windows, illuminated the edge of something ghastly white—a mask. Porcelain, with intricate webbing of hairline cracks across its surface. The figure's head tilted, the mask's eerie smile catching the light in a grotesque greeting.

Katie's throat constricted, silencing the scream that fought to burst forth. Her mind screamed denials, clamoring against the stark, chilling reality before her. Yet the figure lingered, a palpable presence, its obscured gaze heavy on her skin, a suffocating truth in the haunted daylight.

Something skittered across Katie's foot. She recoiled with a sharp yelp, nearly losing her balance in her heels. A mouse, a flurry of frantic energy, darted between her legs, its claws screeching against the warped floorboards as it vanished into the shadows beneath the baseboard.

Her heart was a wild drum solo in her chest as she whirled back to the corner, but the masked figure had evaporated. The dining room was now just a hollow void, dust motes twirling lazily in the weak sunlight that fought through the grime-smeared windows.

"This isn't happening," Katie hissed under her breath, pressing her palms against her throbbing temples. "You're letting this goddamn house get into your head—"

BOOM!

The front door slammed with explosive force, the shockwave rattling the mansion's bones, dislodging decades of dust from the ceiling. The blast echoed through the foyer like a gunshot, sending a piercing ring through Katie's ears.

"No, no, no..." She dashed toward the door, her heels hammering a frantic beat against the floor.

She wrestled with the brass handle, but it was un-yielding, mocking her efforts. With a grunt, she slammed her shoulder against the solid oak, but it might as well have been a fortress wall.

Her fingers clawed at the locks that Paul had pointed out earlier, but they remained stubbornly fixed.

Then, slicing through the tense air, a high-pitched giggle echoed, bouncing off the walls in a disorienting spiral. The sound skittered along her spine—a childlike laugh, yet horribly distorted, as if twisted by a malevolent hand.

"Fuck this." With a swift motion, Katie kicked off her heels, her resolve steeling. She bolted for the grand staircase. There had to be another escape—a second-floor window free from bars, anything.

CRACK!

A step betrayed her, rotten wood splintering un-der her weight. Her stomach plummeted as the world dropped away, and she crashed through, pain exploding in her palms and knees as they collided with jagged boards. Sharp splinters drove into her flesh, painting streaks of red along her skin.

That eerie giggle pierced the air again, now chillingly close, enveloping her in a cacophony of deranged joy. Katie scrambled up, agony ripping through her as she ignored the searing stings in her hands and the tattered remains of her stockings. Blood mingled with dust on her shins, unnoticed.

As the laughter dwindled into a haunting silence, only Katie's ragged breathing filled the desolate mansion, her heartbeats echoing in the oppressive emptiness.

Katie's legs quaked as she staggered away from the crumbling staircase, leaving a trail of bloodied footprints on the warped floorboards. Each throb of the cuts on her palms pulsed in cruel harmony with her frantic heartbeat. Her eyes darted to the shadows that seemed to squirm and contort at the edges of her vision.

The atmosphere thickened oppressively, pressing against her skin as though she were wading through a viscous fog. Dust particles twisted into impossible patterns in the air, forming ephemeral shapes that dissolved whenever she attempted to focus on them. The pervasive silence of the mansion was punctuated only by the mournful creaks of its bones and Katie's labored breaths.

Suddenly, a shadow peeled itself from the darkness behind her. Whirling around, Katie's scream choked off as a porcelain mask emerged from the gloom, its surface veined with hairline cracks that warped its smile into a grotesque sneer. Matted tendrils of dark hair framed the mask like a decayed halo.

With a jarring burst of speed, the figure closed the distance. Sharp nails scraped across Katie's face, the pain explosive and raw. She screamed, her hands flailing up in defense, but the masked woman's grasp was merciless, her nails sinking deeper into Katie's flesh with predatory precision.

Katie's legs flailed, her stockinged feet slipping on the polished floor. The mask hovered inches from her face, the cracks seeming to writhe in the dim light, its hideous grin expanding as if to swallow her whole.

Her cries reverberated off the mansion's cold walls, morphing into strangled sobs as the nails shredded her cheeks. Blood streamed warmly down her face, staining her blazer. Through the haze of tears, she glimpsed the cold metallic shine of a blade.

In a horrific instant, the knife swept across her throat. Katie's knees buckled, her body crumpling to the floor as her blood flowed freely, seeping into the thirsty wood beneath her.

As darkness edged her vision, a soft, childlike humming caressed her fading senses. The last sight that imprinted on her mind was the cracked porcelain mask tilting curiously, those void-like eyes observing her demise.

The humming persisted, a morose lullaby that echoed through the desolate halls, filling the silence that fell thick and heavy once again over the mansion.

Hehl's Threshold

T he autumn mist soaked into Nichols' jacket as he glanced at his watch yet again. Six-thirty. Everything was right on time, yet a knot of unease tightened in his stomach. He watched the crew spill out from the white van, each member hauling out equipment with varying degrees of care.

"Careful with that, it's worth a fortune!" Nichols' command sliced through the crisp air as Tadd wrestled a case of surveying tools from the van's guts.

"Chill, boss. I've got it under control." Tadd's reply was casual as he adjusted his grip on the case, his designer boots crunching on the gravel. "Though, gotta admit, this shithole looks like it's a cough away from crumbling. Sure we should even bother?"

Nichols shot him a glare but said nothing, turning instead to watch Dee efficiently organize his tool belt. At least someone was taking this seriously. Dee caught his look and nodded sharply in acknowledgment.

Jaime climbed out of the passenger side, her red-streaked hair a stark contrast against the drab backdrop of the mansion. She stretched, revealing a sliver of ink under her t-shirt. "This place has got some charm, if you squint."

"That's one way to put it." Jess maneuvered past them, her tablet in hand, already scouting the best angles for exterior shots. Her motions were calculated, utterly professional.

Tadd's laughter cut through the morning stillness. "Yo, Josh! Twenty bucks says there's a ghost in there ready to haunt your ass."

Josh, engrossed with his electrical gear, didn't even look up. "Save your money."

Micah lingered by the van, her phone glued to her hand, her gaze locked on the mansion's foreboding windows. Her fingers danced over the touchscreen, fast and nervous.

Nichols raised his voice, overriding Tadd's ramblings about horror flicks. "We've got maybe an hour of light left. Initial sweep only—check structural integrity, electrical, and foundation. Stick together, no stupid risks. Everyone clear?"

"Crystal, cap'n," Tadd tossed back a mock salute.

They headed for the rusted gates, bags slung over shoulders. Tadd halted, pointing at a tarnished brass plaque on one of the pillars.

"Check it—'Hehl Estate.' That's pronounced 'Hell,' right?" He smirked. "Pretty damn appropriate."

Jess shot him a glare. "It's German, Tadd."

"Still appropriate."

Nichols snapped, "Tadd, focus."

Tadd raised his hands in mock surrender, the smirk lingering. Nichols suppressed a sigh. It was shaping up to be one hell of a long day.

The crunch of gravel resonated under Nichols' boots as he led the way through the overgrown path toward the mansion, its decay more evident with each step.

"Jesus Christ," Dee muttered from behind, his voice a mix of awe and disgust. "This place is straight out of a fucking horror movie."

Nichols' gaze swept over the mansion's facade. Ivy strangled the classical columns, nature's slow, relentless siege on human craftsmanship. The windows, secured with rusted bars, reflected the dimming evening light, broken and distorted like the surface of a disturbed pond. The bars seemed to bow outward, hinting at desperate attempts from within to escape to the outside world.

Noting Katie's Tesla parked out front, Nichols figured she was networking locally, a smart move considering her childhood ties to the area.

"This is some serial killer shit," Tadd remarked, his boot nudging a shattered statue.

"Watch it," Nichols snapped. "Every piece of this goes on record."

Jess, ever the professional, cataloged the exterior damage with her tablet, her camera shutter clicking methodically. Her focus was a steady undercurrent to their tense exploration.

They reached the foreboding entrance, a massive oak door aged by time. Nichols grasped the tarnished handle and pushed; the door moaned open, releasing a gust of stale, musty air so foul it nearly made him retch.

"Inside, now," he commanded, his voice echoing through the cavernous foyer. "Jess, get everything. Everyone else, stick together."

Their flashlights sliced through the darkness, revealing the interior decay—peeling wallpaper, debris littering the floor, and a thick layer of dust that danced like poison in their beams. The grand staircase was an intimidating presence, leading into deeper shadows, its bannister twisted and warped.

Finding a light switch by the door, Nichols flipped it hopefully. The chandelier overhead stuttered to life, its ancient bulbs struggling to illuminate the space, throwing weak, yellowish light that scarcely penetrated the thick gloom. Shadows pooled and pulsed with menace under the sporadic flickers.

"Power's still on," Josh noted, his voice low as he examined his multimeter. "But it's all ancient. Needs a total overhaul."

Nichols nodded, scribbling notes on his clipboard. The quicker they completed this initial survey, the better. Every minute inside the mansion tightened the coil of unease in his stomach, a feeling he'd learned never to ignore.

Nichols' flashlight swept through the foyer, his beam illuminating every imperfection in the grand space—water stains that marred the walls and cobwebs that clung to the chandelier, turning its crystals into spectral prisms. His team fanned out, their lights skittering across the decay like nervous spiders.

Jess's gasp sliced through the silence, her fingers gripping Nichols' arm, her skin ghostly pale in the beam of her flashlight. "Did you see that?" she hissed, her voice just above a whisper. "By the stairs—something moved."

Nichols' eyes darted to the grand staircase where shadows gathered like dark watcr, their edges blurring and shifting with the chandelier's flickers. Nothing stirred now.

"It's just the lights messing with us," he reassured her, though his own heart betrayed him, thudding a frantic rhythm. "Place has been dead for years."

Jaime, who'd been poking around a fractured banister, let out a derisive snort. "Hope we're not kicking off with ghost tales. This dump's got enough bad vibes without—"

Her quip was abruptly severed as she ventured down the hall. "You guys need to see this!" Her shout echoed, her flashlight's beam jittering off the decrepit walls.

Nichols signaled the crew to follow. They trailed Jaime into what appeared to have once been a sitting room, finding her transfixed by a grotesque tableau on a rotting side table.

The sight clawed at Nichols' gut—a macabre arrangement of mummified rats, each adorned with a miniature porcelain mask. The masks mirrored classical theater expressions, their joy and sorrow grotesquely out of place on the tiny, decayed bodies.

"What the actual fuck?" Dee leaned in, his bravado dissolving into palpable disquiet.

Micah's voice broke slightly. "They're... posed. Like some fucked-up art project."

Nichols worked to steady his tone, the air thick with the stench of ancient death and deeper madness. "Document this, Jess. Don't touch a damn thing."

Jess's camera snapped furiously as she circled the grim display. Each flash of her camera threw harsh light on morbid details—tiny ribbons binding shriveled limbs, bits of lace draped over the corpses like ghoulish veils.

Nichols navigated a path through the debris of scattered papers and shattered glass, his team trailing behind him into the dense gloom of the mansion. At the end of the long, oppressive hallway, the study's double doors loomed, barely clinging to rusted hinges. His flashlight sliced through the darkness, revealing rich oak paneling and towering bookshelves, their once ordered contents now a chaotic spread across the buckled floorboards.

"Fan out," he commanded, his voice echoing slightly. "Document everything, but be damn careful where you step."

The musty stench of mildew hung heavy in the air, mixing with the omnipresent scent of decay. Dust lay thick upon every surface, undisturbed until now. Dominating the room was a massive desk, its dark wood marred with scars and stains from water damage. Papers and leather-bound books surrounded it, tossed aside in a wild disarray as though the room had been violently searched.

Jess's attention was drawn to a leather-bound volume amidst the clutter. She abandoned her camera, curiosity piqued, and picked up the diary, the yellowed pages fluttering under her fingers.

"It's a diary," she announced, her voice laden with tension as her fingers traced the faded script. "It belonged to... Mimi Hehl."

Tadd's laughter, nervous and mocking, reverberated against the somber walls. "Great, just what we need—creepy-ass diaries in haunted mansions. This will end well."

Nichols moved closer, an uneasy sensation clawing at him. It felt wrong, like they were trespassing into a realm of privacy so deep it was almost sacred.

As the others huddled around, Jess's hands trembled slightly under the harsh beam of Nichols' flashlight as she turned the brittle pages.

"Listen to this," she murmured, eyes narrowing as she deciphered the spidery handwriting. "'Mother says we must stay inside now. The town has turned against us. They whisper that we brought the sickness, that we're cursed. But Mother knows the truth—we're the chosen ones. We alone will survive what's coming.'"

Micah hugged herself, her voice a whisper. "When was this written?"

"Early 2020," Jess replied, her fingers hesitantly flipping to the next page. "During the pandemic lockdowns."

Dee leaned in, his voice a low murmur. "Man, this family was twisted."

Jess's voice grew more strained as she continued. "'Mother's experiments are progressing. She says the masks will protect us, keep the corruption from seeping into our souls. I watch her work in the basement, preserving what she calls her 'specimens.' The needles gleam in the candlelight. Sometimes I hear singing from below, but when I ask, Mother says it's just the house speaking to us.'"

Josh shifted, unease flickering across his face. "Maybe we should just leave this stuff alone."

Nichols was about to agree when Jess turned another page, gasping sharply. The room leaned in.

The diary's yellowed pages were filled with crude sketches—masks drawn in what seemed like dried blood, twisted into horrific expressions. Among these drawings, figures danced wildly, their limbs distorted in unnatural poses, some adorned with masks, others mere empty shells of form, stripped of any humanity.

"Jesus," Jaime breathed, stepping back as if the pages themselves were cursed.

The drawings grew increasingly chaotic, the strokes deeper, more desperate. Between the grotesque images, words were scrawled in a frenzied hand: "KEEP US SAFE," "MOTHER KNOWS BEST," "THEY MUST WEAR THE MASKS."

Nichols slammed the diary shut, his fingers staining the dusty cover. The sun's feeble rays struggled against the filth on the windows, casting elongated shadows that crawled across the study's battered floor. Every nerve in his body screamed for him to end the day's explorations, but the hardened pragmatist in him—the part honed by two decades on the job—pushed those instincts aside.

"We need a thorough sweep before tomorrow," he declared, his voice slicing through the heavy air. "The faster we document everything, the faster we can get the hell out of here."

"You can't be serious." Jess's voice shook, her tablet quivering in her grasp. "After what we just uncovered—"

"It's just a diary from a troubled family during a lockdown." Nichols's tone was unyielding, meant to brook no argument. "That's all."

Tadd's uneasy chuckle scraped on Nichols' already frayed nerves. "Yeah, nothing like a little bedtime story about masks and mummified rats. Totally normal pandemic shit."

"Enough, Tadd." Nichols flashed his flashlight over the group, settling on each face. "Josh, Dee—basement. Jess, Jaime—the kitchen. Micah, you're on upstairs fixtures. Jess—"

"I'm not heading up alone," Micah blurted, her voice tinged with panic.

"Fine. Pair up with Jess and Jaime. Tadd, you're with me. We're hitting the dining room."

The group disbanded with reluctance. Nichols noted Jess's backward glances towards the foyer, her posture tense. Catching her eye, he gave her a firm nod, silently urging her to hold it together. She straightened and followed Micah with determined steps.

"Just the two of us, boss." Tadd tried for nonchalance, but his voice betrayed him. "Ready for this gourmet experience?"

Nichols led them down the corridor, his boots imprinting on the thick layer of dust. The dining room doors protested as he pushed them open, their hinges screaming with neglect.

The room unfolded into shadow, vast and looming. Their flashlights cut across an ancient dining table set for twenty, the wood lackluster under layers of grime. Crystal decanters glinted dully, their spirits long since evaporated. Chairs were scattered as if abandoned mid-meal.

"Check the walls for water damage," Nichols instructed, his voice low. "And try not to wreck anything else."

"Sir, yes, sir," Tadd responded, sarcasm lacing his tone yet undercut by his palpable unease.

The atmosphere thickened, oppressive and dense against Nichols' skin. Their footsteps echoed oddly, each sound lingering too long as if reluctant to fade. Shadows seemed to pulse at the edge of his vision, a dark presence brushing against the edges of reality.

A whisper floated through the stillness, so soft Nichols almost dismissed it.

"Did you hear that?" Tadd's voice cracked, startling them both.

"Probably just the wind," Nichols replied, though the stagnant air mocked his words.

Somewhere in the mansion, a door made an unnerving creaking sound. Nichols tightened his grip on the flashlight, his jaw clenched as he suppressed a rising tide of fear. They were professionals, he reminded himself sternly. They had a job to do.

But when another whisper snaked through the darkness, even his staunch pragmatism couldn't ignore the dread that this place—this job—was profoundly, disturbingly wrong.

FLICKERING DEMISE

J osh adjusted the beam of his flashlight, testing its strength against the darkness looming ahead. The basement door stood before them, its surface marred by deep, violent scratches, as if something had desperately sought escape. He glanced at Dee, noticing the tension in his shoulders, reminiscent of a boxer bracing for the first bell.

"You think we'll run into any of that freaky shit from the diary down here?" Dee's voice held a trace of genuine concern, a stark contrast to his usual bravado.

Josh shook his head, gripping the schematic of the electrical panel tighter in his other hand. "Nah, just the usual suspects—old wires and rats." The reassurance rang hollow, even to his own ears, but it was all he had to cling to in the face of the unknown.

Dee pushed tentatively against the door as it creaked open slowly, revealing a staircase that descended into utter blackness. The steps moaned under their weight as they made their descent, the decrepit state of the staircase mirroring the decay that clung to the very air. Josh's flashlight flickered across the walls, illuminating water stains that morphed into ghastly faces and cracks that branched out like the limbs of a tortured tree.

As they went deeper, the air thickened, chilling their breaths and carrying a metallic tang that clawed at Josh's throat. It was eerily reminiscent of blood—a stark, coppery scent that brought back unwanted memories of past injuries.

"This smell isn't right," Josh muttered, his voice a low echo in the oppressive darkness. The words seemed to dissipate as soon as they left his lips, absorbed by the hungry gloom.

Dee's smirk was forced, his usual swagger faltering as his gaze flickered anxiously through the shadows. "Scared of a little basement stench?" he quipped, though the edge to his tone betrayed his unease.

Then, it came—a whisper so subtle, Josh almost convinced himself it was his imagination. But there was no mistaking the soft, sinister murmur that floated up from the deeper shadows, brushing against his ears like a caress from the grave.

His feet rooted to the spot, his pulse hammering in his ears as cold dread seeped into his bones. He strained to listen, every fiber of his being praying it was just a trick of the mind. But the basement's silence was now a menacing void, waiting to be filled by whispers from the dark.

Josh's flashlight beam trembled as they descended onto the basement floor, where long shadows sprawled across the damp concrete like dark fingers. The metallic odor intensified, tightening around his throat like a noose. Somewhere in the gloom, water dripped relentlessly, each drop resonating like a hammer strike in the silent, oppressive air.

"Check this out," Dee murmured, his flashlight revealing a heavy wooden door set deeply into the far wall. The air grew colder as they approached.

Josh edged closer, his steps cautious on the slick floor. Deep gouges scarred the door's surface, violent marks that spoke of desperate efforts to escape. A rusted padlock, pitted with the corrosion of time, dangled from the latch, mocking their presence with its stubborn endurance.

Dee traced the scratches with a finger, his voice a half-whisper. "Looks like whatever was in here was damn desperate to get out." His attempt at humor faltered, swallowed by the stale air. "Reckon this is where they kept those 'specimens'?"

His gaze lingered on Dee, who now pulled a crowbar from his belt, the metal dull under the scant light. "Think you can crack it open?" Josh asked, his voice betraying a flicker of dread.

"Watch and learn," Dee grunted, sliding the crowbar against the lock and applying a formidable force. The lock resisted with a groan but didn't give.

As Dee persisted, Josh swept his flashlight around the room, illuminating shelves crammed with glass jars that lined the walls. Each jar contained forms suspended in murky liquid—shapes too distorted and grotesque for Josh to fully discern or understand.

Then his beam caught something chilling in the corner: a mannequin, garbed in what looked like a decaying wedding dress, the fabric yellowed and hanging in shreds. Its face was smooth, devoid of features except for two dark cavities where eyes should have been. Josh's stomach churned—those hollow sockets seemed to follow him, a silent accusation.

The sudden clang of metal on metal made Josh's heart leap to his throat. He whipped around to see Dee discarding the crowbar in frustration.

"Damn thing's solid," Dee said, wiping his brow with the back of his hand, defeat etched across his face.

Josh turned his attention to the electrical panel on the wall, intent on completing their original task. As he moved, something brushed against his face—thin, clinging strands that wrapped around him with an eerie persistence. He recoiled, swatting at the invisible tendrils.

"Spider web got you?" Dee chuckled, finding humor in his discomfort. "You should see how you look right now."

Josh scrubbed at his face, removing the last of the web with trembling hands. "We should head back up. I've seen enough horrors for one day."

"Couldn't agree more," Dee said, retrieving his crowbar and giving the padlocked door a final, resigned glance.

They turned towards the stairs, their steps hastening instinctively as they left the basement's morbid secrets behind them, each echo of their footsteps a reminder of the unsettling depths they were eager to escape.

Jess's flashlight sliced through the kitchen's oppressive gloom, uncovering years of abandonment in its harsh light. Cobwebs hung from the cabinet handles like shrouds of tattered lace, and a filthy patina clung to every surface. Her boots crunched on shards of glass and debris as she ventured deeper into the culinary wasteland.

"This place is a goddamn health inspector's horror show." Jaime's voice cut through the thick air as she wrenched open a drawer, unleashing a cloud of dust that swirled around them. Rusted utensils clanked together, their handles warped and stained.

Near the doorway, Micah hunched over, her hands rifling through a pile of decaying papers. "These look like recipes, but..." She squinted at the blurred handwriting. "Who the hell uses formaldehyde in soup?"

"Someone with a fucked-up palate," Jess muttered, pulling open a cabinet to reveal rows of empty mason jars. Dark residues marred the insides, and the peeling labels hinted at long-forgotten contents. The smell hit them next—a vile, sweet rot that twisted Jess's gut.

"Holy shit," Micah gasped, her voice cracking. "What is that stench?"

"Probably just some dead rats in the walls," Jaime suggested with a hollow smirk, rapping her knuckles against the crumbling wallpaper. "Or the last owners left something behind to evolve into new life forms."

"Not funny," Micah shot back, her face twisted in disgust.

The foul odor intensified as Jess approached the old stove, where a massive cast-iron pot sat, its exterior crusted with rust and a darker substance. Her hand shook as she reached for the lid.

"What the hell is that?" Micah's voice trembled, her body tensed for retreat yet drawn forward by a morbid curiosity.

"Let's find out," Jess said, her voice just above a whisper. She gripped the lid with her gloved hand, lifting it slowly. The scrape of metal on metal seemed to echo a warning as she unveiled the ghastly contents: the mummified remains of a cat, contorted unnaturally, its fur reduced to a leather-like sheath tightly stretched over sharp bones. Precision cuts crisscrossed its corpse—surgical and deliberate, the stitches meticulously placed in its dried flesh.

"Jesus Christ," Jess murmured, her throat tight as she stared at the macabre display. Each cut was executed with chilling exactness, revealing a twisted intent that churned her stomach.

Micah's scream ripped through the silence, her body recoiling into the cabinets with a loud thud as her hand clamped over her mouth. The sound echoed, multiplying in the empty mansion and returning as a terrifying chorus.

Footsteps thundered in the hallway, growing louder as they neared. Tadd burst into the kitchen first, his usual bravado washed away, replaced by raw alarm. His eyes swept the room, landing on their pale faces and the open pot.

"What the fuck happened?" His voice was thick with panic, his chest heaving as if he'd run from a nightmare.

Jess's heart raced as Tadd's question reverberated through the stale kitchen air. Jaime, her complexion ashen, extended a trembling hand toward the cast iron pot, its grim contents now the center of their collective horror.

"See for yourself," she croaked, her voice little more than a whisper.

Tadd moved closer, his designer boots crunching over the scattered debris. He peered into the pot, then jerked back violently. "Fuck me," he gasped, staggering into the counter. "That's straight out of a serial killer's playbook."

Nichols, Josh, and Dee stormed into the room, their heavy boots thudding against the old floorboards, faces slick with sweat from their dash up from the basement.

"What's going on? We heard screaming," Nichols demanded, his tone slicing through the tension.

Jess stepped back, allowing him closer to the grim discovery. As his flashlight beam illuminated the grotesque spectacle of the preserved cat, its face was contorted in a snarl, more menacing under the harsh light.

"Probably some twisted kid's idea of a prank," Nichols muttered, grabbing a knife from the counter. "Let's see how real—"

Suddenly, the cat's head snapped towards him with a chilling swiftness, jaws clacking shut mere inches from his fingers. A horrifying, hybrid sound—a cross between a hiss and a shriek—erupted from its throat. The pot tipped over with a deafening crash, spilling the cat's mangled form onto the floor, its limbs twisted, stitches popping from its dried skin.

"Holy shit!" Dee recoiled, slamming into Josh.

Micah clung to Jess, her nails digging painfully through the fabric of Jess's sleeve. Her body shook violently as she pressed closer. The air turned thick with the stench of decay, nearly tangible in its intensity.

The overhead lights flickered once, then again, more violently. Darkness descended swiftly, engulfing them in an oppressive, tangible blackness.

"Fuck this!" Tadd's voice cracked, laced with raw fear. "We need to get the hell out!"

Cell phones flickered weakly in the dark, their pale glow futile against the engulfing shadows. Jess fumbled with her own phone, her fingers shaking as she attempted to dial 911—useless. The screen mocked her with its empty signal bar.

"Anyone got a signal?" Josh's voice floated through the darkness, met only with negative murmurs.

The oppressive darkness seemed to pulse around them, heavy, almost sentient. From somewhere in the depths of the kitchen, the unmistakable sound of something scratching against the floor resonated, adding a primal fear to the already frantic atmosphere.

Jess's heart pounded like a drumline in her chest as she raced towards the foyer, her boots slamming against the warped floorboards. The beam of her flashlight flitted across peeling wallpaper and dusty portraits, casting erratic shadows that churned her stomach. The frantic sounds of ragged breathing and pounding footsteps echoed behind her, punctuating the thick darkness of the corridor.

They exploded into the foyer, their flashlight beams slicing through the gloom, crisscrossing like desperate searchlights. Shadows writhed across the walls, twisting the mundane into monstrous forms. Jess swept her light across the room, her hands shaking violently.

Nichols lunged for the front door, muscles tensed, and seized the handle. The metal rattled under his fierce grip, but the door refused to yield. "It's locked," he growled, the edge of frustration biting through the tension in his voice.

Dee dashed to the nearest window, his flashlight revealing the grim reality of iron bars firmly set. "Fuck, fuck, fuck!" His fist pounded against the wall, the sound of his despair echoing starkly. "These bars aren't moving."

"This is complete bullshit!" Tadd's outburst filled the foyer as he slammed his fists against the heavy door, his designer boots scuffing the floor with each futile kick.

Josh swept his flashlight around the entrance, his breathing sharp and rapid. "Our gear... it's all gone. Everything's fucking gone."

A chill sliced through Jess as realization dawned; their pile of tools and equipment, earlier placed neatly by the door, had disappeared without a trace. Her mind whirled, grappling with the inexplicable— the grotesque discovery in the kitchen, their vanished equipment, the immovable door. Nothing made sense.

Then, slicing through their collective panic, the sound of footsteps echoed from above—heavy, deliberate, each thud reverberating through the ceiling with chilling precision. They froze, their lights stabbing upwards towards the second-floor landing. Jess held her breath, her body tensed for any sound.

"Tell me you heard that," Jaime whispered, her voice trembling on the verge of hysteria.

A laugh, high and haunting, wove through the stillness, seeming to emanate from the shadows themselves. The eerie sound skittered across Jess's skin, raising goosebumps in its wake. Her voice was tight as she choked out a name, "Katie?"

"That's not Katie," Nichols responded with certainty, his tone cutting through the darkness, brooking no argument.

The footsteps resumed overhead, deliberate and taunting, sending a cascade of dust drifting down like malignant snow. Jess's flashlight caught the swirling particles, creating an ethereal barrier between them and the unseen menace lurking above. The tense silence hung heavily, suffused with dread and the echo of that mocking laughter, as they stood, trapped and helpless, in the shadowed foyer.

In the dim glow of her flashlight, Jess watched, powerless, as Jaime hurled herself at the nearest window, her fists beating futilely against the glass. The iron bars cast stark, jail-like shadows across her face, distorting her expression into one of primal fear.

"Help! Somebody help us!" Jaime's voice broke through the silence with desperate, raw edges. Her cries echoed into the emptiness outside, only to be swallowed by the vast darkness. No lights flickered to life in the nearby houses, no faces appeared at the windows—only an unending void stretched out into the night.

"Everyone needs to stay calm," Nichols commanded, his voice slicing through the escalating hysteria, though Jess detected the underlying strain. His attempt to impose order seemed only to ignite the tension further.

"How the fuck did the doors lock?" Dee's voice was sharp, accusatory as he turned on Josh. "You were the last one near them!"

Josh's face twisted with offense. "Are you kidding me? I was down in the basement with you the whole damn time!"

"Then who—"

"Stop it!" Nichols's shout cut above the fray, but his command barely dented the spiraling chaos.

Jess's gaze shifted to Micah, huddled against the wall, small whimpers escaping her as tears carved clear paths through the dust on her cheeks. Her body trembled with each quiet sob, her hands gripping the peeling wallpaper for support.

"Oh, for fuck's sake." Jaime's scorn was palpable as she abandoned the window. "Are you seriously crying right now, Micah? Real helpful."

Micah's tearful eyes hardened, her grief swiftly morphing into anger. "At least I'm not the one screaming like a lunatic and telling whatever's up there exactly where we are!"

Their bickering was abruptly overshadowed by a resurgence of laughter—higher, closer this time, its mocking timbre tinged with cruelty, echoing off the walls and enveloping them. Jess felt a chill as the sound seemed to coil around them, tangible and menacing.

Tadd's flashlight beam danced frantically, reflecting his shaking hands. "Shit, shit, shit," he murmured

under his breath, his voice a trembling mantra of fea
r.

A dark blur swept across the hallway entrance, its movement too swift, too fluid to be human. Jess's pulse surged with adrenaline, her instincts screaming danger.

"We need to stick together," she found herself saying, her voice a surprising bastion of calm in the chaos. "Staying here just makes us easy targets."

Nichols gave a terse nod, his features set in a grim line of resolve. "This way," he directed, leading them deeper into the bowels of the house, away from the exposed and vulnerable foyer.

LAUGHTER IN THE BLOOD

J osh's heart pounded a relentless rhythm against his ribs as he trailed behind the group, moving through the mansion's shadow-laden hallway. His flashlight's beam illuminated patches of peeling wallpaper and exposed beams, the light casting sinister shadows that writhed like specters against the walls. Despite the chill seeping from the mansion's aged stones, sweat ran coldly down his neck, a stark contrast to the fear tightening his chest.

"We need to find another way out," Nichols commanded from the front, his voice a strained whisper of forced calm. "There has to be a service entrance or—"

A high-pitched giggle sliced through the silence, chilling and clear.

Josh whipped around, his flashlight slicing through the darkness behind them. "Did anyone else hear that?" His voice was tight, the words just squeezing past the constriction in his throat.

Dee glanced back, his face etched with fatigue and shadow. "Probably just the wind, man. This place is old as hell."

But Josh felt a deep, unsettling certainty—it wasn't the wind. The sound was too precise, too intentional. It echoed the haunting laughter they'd heard earlier, the memory of which still clawed at his nerves with its vividness. The recollection of the deeply gouged wood in the basement door sent a shiver down his spine, reigniting the fear that flickered like a shadow in his mind.

The group's footsteps reverberated through the corridor, a stark soundtrack to their tense advance. Lagging behind, Josh kept his flashlight trained on the darkness they had just traversed. Another giggle, undeniably closer now, froze him in place. It emanated from a slightly ajar door just to his right.

"Hey," he called out in a hushed tone, but his voice was swallowed by the distance as the others rounded a corner, their lights dimming in the expanding distance between them.

The door before him creaked, as if inviting him closer with an eerie sound. Rational thought urged him to follow the safety of the group, but an inexplicable pull drew him toward the darkened room. "Hello?" he ventured, his voice low and cautious, as he stepped closer to the gap, his heart racing with a mix of dread and an uncontrollable draw to uncover what lay beyond.

Josh's hand trembled as he swept the flashlight beam across the room, dust motes swirling chaotically in the weak light. The beam exposed peeling floral wallpaper and water-stained ceiling tiles, hinting at years of neglect. A musty draft caressed the back of his neck, drawing his gaze to an anomaly in the far wall—a corner that jutted out at an unusual angle, creating a seam that whispered of hidden secrets.

"What the hell?" he murmured to himself.

Curiosity piqued, Josh pressed his hand against the cold, off-kilter panel. It yielded slightly under his touch. With a firmer push, the wall groaned open on rusted hinges, releasing a blast of stale, metallic-scented air that assaulted his senses, making him gag.

A dark passage loomed before him, devouring the weak beam of his flashlight. Every instinct screamed for him to turn back, to seek the safety of numbers, but the mysterious pull that had drawn him here now nudged him deeper into the unknown.

He advanced hesitantly, his boots crunching over unseen debris. His flashlight revealed makeshift shelves carved into the rock walls, laden with jars filled with murky, unidentifiable contents. Josh forced himself not to dwell on what they might hold.

The passage ended abruptly in a small chamber. The flashlight beam settled on what appeared to be a figure seated in an ancient wooden chair against

the far wall. At first glance, it looked like a mannequin, placed in a pose of eerie contemplation.

Josh edged closer, the dim light gradually revealing the horrifying truth. This was no dummy.

The corpse in the chair was dressed in tattered
remnants, its head drooping unnaturally forward. As
the light washed over it, the reality hit Josh like a
physical blow. The skin was waxy, unnaturally tight
across the skeleton beneath, the eyes hollow, the
jaw agape in a silent, eternal scream of terror or a
gony.

"Oh fuck, oh fuck—" Panic surged as he stumbled
back, the flashlight slipping from his sweat-slicked
hand and crashing to the ground. The light skittered
away, casting wild shadows before settling.

Then, a soft, chilling giggle cut through the silence.

Josh froze, his breath sharp in his throat. The
sound was unmistakably close—a childlike laugh
that twisted his stomach into knots.

"Who's playing hide and seek?" The voice was
sing-song, malicious in its innocence. "I found yo
u..."

He lunged for the flashlight, heart pounding,
and spun around. The beam caught a glimpse of
white—a cracked porcelain mask floating in the
darkness. The figure stepped forward gracefully, its
head cocked in a macabre tilt. In her hand, she bran-
dished a syringe filled with a clear liquid, catching
the dim light and sending a shiver down Josh's spine.

His voice caught in his throat as the masked figure—Mimi, or what once was Mimi—looked at him

through the empty eye sockets of the mask. The reality of the nightmare before him was paralyzing, the implications horrifying beyond belief.

Josh's heart slammed against his ribcage as his gaze fixated on the porcelain mask, its surface marred by jagged cracks that caught the dim light, twisting the hollow smile into something sinister and alive. Panic surged through his veins, his muscles tensed for flight, yet terror cemented his feet to the ground.

"Stay the fuck back!" he barked, his voice cracking under the strain, raw with fear.

Mimi advanced, each step deliberate and fluid, the syringe in her hand glinting with menace as the clear liquid within it sloshed with threat. Josh's mind spiraled with nightmarish thoughts of what horrors the syringe might contain. His eyes frantically scanned the room for any semblance of a weapon.

His gaze landed on a wooden chair against the wall, its frame aged and cloaked in dust. With a desperate lunge, he grasped it, feeling the coarse, brittle wood under his palms. With a guttural yell, he hurled it with all his might towards Mimi.

The chair arced through the air, crashing into the wall and shattering into pieces as Mimi sidestepped with eerie agility. Her head cocked at an unnatural angle, a chilling giggle escaping her lips.

"No, no, no—" Josh's voice was a panicked whisper. He snatched a heavy leather-bound book from a nearby table and threw it with trembling hands. It struck her shoulder, a feeble attempt that did nothing to alter her steady, menacing approach.

A misstep sent him tumbling backward, his heel snagging on a loose floorboard. The world spun wildly as he fell, his head striking the ground with a sickening thud. Pain erupted through his skull, blurring his vision. The flashlight skidded from his grasp, its beam careening wildly, casting grotesque shadows that leaped along the walls.

Panic clawed at his throat as he scrambled backwards, his hands scraping painfully across the splintered wood. Mimi loomed over him, her movements smooth and terrifyingly precise. The hollow eyes of the mask stared down at him, the distorted giggle resonating in the confined space.

"Time for your medicine," she cooed, her voice a twisted sing-song as she raised the syringe. The gleam of the needle was the last thing Josh saw as he flailed helplessly, his body frozen between the urge to fight and the instinct to flee.

Josh's scream choked in his throat as Mimi's fingers, cold and unyielding, tangled viciously in his hair, wrenching his head back with a force that seemed superhuman. The sharp pain of his scalp stretching seared through him as the cold porcelain of her mask pressed menacingly close to his ear, her breath skimming eerily across his skin.

"Shhh... the medicine will make everything better," she crooned, her voice twisting into a grotesque lullaby. "Just like Mommy used to say."

The syringe loomed in his peripheral vision, its needle catching the dim light. Josh's body thrashed desperately against her iron hold, his actions sluggish and ineffectual, hampered by the disorientation from his earlier fall. His fingers clawed at the decaying wood of the floorboards, scraping helplessly.

"No, please—" His plea was cut short as a white-hot burst of pain shattered through his skull. The needle drove into his eye, burrowing deep. A searing agony surged through his optic nerve, spreading like venom through his brain. His screams devolved into raw, primal howls—the sounds of a man being driven beyond the brink of enduring agony.

Warmth trickled down his cheek—blood mingling with the sinister concoction she had injected. His vision blurred with tears in his remaining eye, distorting the horrific grin fixed on Mimi's mask as it hovered over him.

"More medicine," Mimi's giggle was chilling, detached, as she raised the syringe again. "You're such a good patient."

The needle punctured his neck—once, twice, repeatedly—each stab unleashing new torrents of excruciating pain that ravaged his body. Josh's form convulsed uncontrollably, his limbs flailing in a grotesque dance of agony. His hands fluttered weakly in the air, grasping for salvation that would never come.

"Sweet dreams," Mimi murmured, her mask tilting to one side as if to get a better view of the agony etched across Josh's face. "Time to sleep forever."

Josh's arms dropped lifelessly to his sides, his final breath a labored gasp that filled the chilling silence of the room. Then, stillness claimed him.

The last sound that filled his fading consciousness was Mimi's childlike laughter, a haunting echo that followed him into the dark oblivion.

Jess's heart raced as Josh's harrowing screams tore through the stifling silence of the mansion. Her flashlight sliced through the dark, erratic beams painting the walls as she dashed down the hallway, the heavy footfalls of the others pounding close behind.

"Josh!" Her voice shattered with desperation, raw and hoarse. "Where are you?"

Abruptly, the screams ceased, sucked into a void of heavy breathing and their thunderous steps. Dee and Tadd surged ahead, brushing roughly against the decaying walls as they barreled forward. Jess's flashlight flickered across a door ajar, revealing an unexplored room.

"In here!" The urgency in Dee's voice was something new, tinged with a terror Jess had never heard from him before.

She skidded into the room, her boots slipping on the littered papers that carpeted the dusty floor. The light from her flashlight revealed walls clad in peeling wallpaper and furniture left to the mercy of time. A cold draft slithered through the space, heavy with the metallic tang of blood.

The beam settled on a hidden passage first—an unnatural gap in the wall. Then, horrifyingly, it found Josh.

Bile surged in her throat as she took in the sight. Josh lay crumpled on the floor, his blood spreading out in a sickening halo around his head. His eye socket was a dark, hollow abyss, stark and violent. Needle marks marred his neck, each puncture a brutal dot in a macabre pattern.

"Fuck," Tadd murmured under his breath, his usual cockiness drained from him. "Oh fuck."

Jess clamped a hand over her mouth, stifling the nausea that clawed up her throat. The acrid smell of blood invaded her senses, blending with the dank mustiness of the room. Her fingers quivered against the flashlight's handle as she forced herself to look away from the grotesque sight of Josh's disfigured face.

Then, slicing through the tense air, a giggle—high-pitched and chillingly childish, yet laced with a dark malice—echoed in the room. Jess's skin crawled as the sound prickled her arms. Whipping around, her light briefly caught the outline of a figure donning a cracked porcelain mask, its head tilted in a disturbing angle. But in the blink of an eye, it was gone.

"We need to go," Nichols said, his voice quivering with a fear that matched the rest. "Now."

They retreated from the room, each movement laden with dread. Jess's flashlight sporadically illuminated their stricken faces—pale, eyes wide, features etched with horror. The solidarity they once shared had fragmented under the weight of their terror.

They hastened back into the hallway, leaving behind the ghastly scene in the blood-drenched room. The sinister giggle seemed to chase them, reverberating off the walls in a twisted mockery of their panic.

Fractured Alliances

J ess's flashlight beam quivered across the parlor, illuminating the remnants of its once splendid decor. Shattered glass crunched under Tadd's boots as he paced restlessly, his movements sending sharp, echoing sounds through the heavy silence. The metallic stench of Josh's blood lingered in the air, a constant reminder of their vulnerability, twisting Jess's stomach with nausea.

"We can't just sit here doing nothing," Nichols declared, his voice betraying a rare edge of desperation as his gaze flicked nervously between the darkened corridors that stretched away from the parlor.

Jess's throat felt tight, her voice strained but determined as she responded. "We don't even know what we're dealing with."

Behind her, Jaime and Micah huddled together, their rapid breaths punctuating the tense silence. Jess's flashlight swept across Dee, who was propped against a broken bookshelf, his face taut, hands clenched so tightly his knuckles shone pale in the dim light.

"We don't know?" Dee's voice was sharp, cutting through the stifling air as he straightened up, stepping away from the shadowed shelves. "It's one psycho in a mask. We find her, and we end this nightmare."

"Yeah, because that worked out so great for Josh." Tadd's voice was laden with a mix of sarcasm and fear, his foot lashing out to send a shard of glass skittering noisily across the floor. His restless movements seemed to punctuate the hopelessness of their situation, each step echoed unsettlingly throughout the once grand parlor.

Micah's fingers twisted in the hem of her sweater, her voice a tremulous whisper. "We should stick together. Splitting up is exactly what—"

"Oh, sure." Jaime's harsh laugh sliced through the darkness, sharp as shattered glass. "Let's just huddle in a corner and wait to die. Great plan, Micah."

Jess clenched her jaw, watching as Micah recoiled, her fear almost tangible in the heavy, musty air mingled with the metallic scent of Josh's blood. Despite the pounding of her own heart, Jess injected a firm resolve into her voice. "Enough! If we keep turning on each other, we're as good as dead."

Her words hung in the stale air, weighted with desperation. Dust motes danced in the beam of her flashlight, catching on the silvery strands of cobwebs that bridged the decaying crown molding. The oppressive silence of the mansion enveloped them, accentuated only by their uneven breathing and Tadd's shuffling feet.

Suddenly, a soft, high-pitched giggle pierced the tension. The sound crawled up Jess's spine, a chilling caress that prickled her skin. She spun around, her flashlight sweeping the room, where shadows seemed to pulse and coil in the corners. The light briefly captured their distorted reflections in the remnants of a shattered window, turning their faces into grotesque caricatures.

"Did anyone else hear that?" Jess's voice echoed in the room, sounding detached and distant.

Tadd exhaled shakily, trying to cloak his fear with humor. "Yeah, no big deal. Just the sound of our impending doom." But the quiver in his voice betrayed his fright.

Nichols's fist tightened, the muscles in his forearm bulging as if ready to strike out at unseen threats. His jaw was set, his gaze fixed intently on the dark maw of the parlor doorway, as if willing the shadows to reveal their secrets.

The giggle reverberated through the hallway again, closer this time, and Jess's heart pounded fiercely against her ribs. Her grip on the flashlight intensified, knuckles whitening with the strain as she swept its beam across the corridor. A shadow flickered between doorways, elusive and swift, a mere whisper of movement that evaded direct sight.

"Fuck this." Dee's voice was a harsh whisper as he stripped off his toolbelt and slammed it down on a dusty side table, the sound of metal clanging against wood reverberating in the tense air. He rummaged through his tools with hurried, determined movements, handing a heavy wrench to Nichols and a crowbar to Tadd. Choosing the largest hammer for himself, he hefted it, his expression set with grim resolve.

Jess watched the men arm themselves, her throat dry, the rational part of her screaming that they were outmatched by whatever horror lurked in the shadows. The gruesome image of Josh's violently altered face—his eye socket a hollow ruin—flashed unbidden into her mind, the memory so vivid it churned her stomach.

"We need to find an exit," she asserted, her voice wobbling with forced authority as she tried to quell the trembling in her hands. She turned to Micah and Jaime, who stood pale and visibly shaking in the weak light. "The three of us can search while you—"

"Take care of the bitch," Nichols interjected, his voice low and fierce, his grip on the wrench tight enough to whiten his knuckles. "You three find a way out. We'll handle this."

Jess nodded, her every instinct screaming against the idea of splitting up, but desperation edged her decision. She motioned to Jaime and Micah, pulling them close as she led the way toward the corridor. Her flashlight cut a swath through the darkness, revealing more of the mansion's decaying interior: peeling wallpaper and water-stained ceilings.

They moved down the winding corridor, each step cautious, the floorboards creaking under their weight with a menacing sound. Jess's nerves were taut, stretched thin by the oppressive silence and the eerie echoes of their own movements. Jaime's breaths were sharp and erratic behind her.

A whisper slithered through the darkness, so soft it might have been conjured by their fears, but it chilled Jess to the core.

Jaime's hand clamped onto Micah's arm, her grip tight. "Did you hear—"

Micah pulled away sharply, her voice cold and hard. "Get your fucking hands off me. I don't need your pretend concern now."

Jess pressed forward, her jaw clenched in determination. She couldn't afford to look back or dwell on the fate of the men they'd left behind. The flashlight in her hand quivered as she shone it ahead, piercing the gloom as they navigated deeper into the unknown. Every part of her was alert, praying they'd find an exit before the nightmare escalated any further.

Tadd's heart was a relentless drum in his chest as he clutched the crowbar, his palms slick with sweat that made the metal handle slippery and unreliable. The beam of his flashlight jittered across peeling wallpaper, casting grotesque shadows that danced and twisted, churning his stomach with unease.

"This is such bullshit," he murmured under his breath, eyes fixed on Dee's broad back as the handyman advanced with a determination Tadd wished he could feel. Hammer poised like a weapon of war, Dee seemed a stark contrast to Tadd's own wavering resolve. Nichols, maintaining a disciplined calm, positioned himself between them, each breath measured and controlled.

Dee's voice shattered the oppressive silence of the corridor. "Come out, you crazy bitch! Let's end this!" His challenge boomed through the hallway, reckless and defiant.

"Real smart," Tadd muttered, his voice a thin, reedy contrast to Dee's thunderous bellow. "Antagonize the psycho who just turned Josh into a human pincushion." Despite his attempt at sarcasm, the words were tinged with fear, stripping any pretense of bravery he might have projected.

As they moved, the floorboards groaned audibly under their weight, sending spikes of anxiety racing up Tadd's spine. The air was thick with the scent of decay and an underlying tang of metal—too reminiscent of blood, Josh's blood—that filled Tadd's mouth with the taste of copper. He swallowed hard, fighting the visceral image of Josh's mutilated body from his mind.

"We should have stayed with the others," he confessed, his voice cracking with vulnerability. "Safety in numbers and all that shit."

"Shut up," Nichols growled back, his grip tightening on the wrench as if preparing for battle.

Then, a sound—like nails dragging across wood—whispered through the darkness ahead. Tadd's breath hitched, fear seizing his lungs. His flashlight swept the corridor, its beam slicing through the murk to reveal nothing but more deserted hall, deepening shadows, endless places for her to hide.

Dee pressed on, his frustration mounting with each cleared doorway. "Where are you hiding?" he bellowed, his voice echoing back at them distorted, as if the house itself mocked their efforts.

Suddenly, the atmosphere shifted; a subtle drop in pressure that made Tadd's ears pop uncomfortably. Above them, the chandelier emitted a pitiful groan, its crystals chiming mournfully.

"Watch out!" Tadd's warning was just in time for Dee to leap forward as the chandelier crashed down behind him, shattering into a cascade of crystal and rust. The sound was catastrophic in the enclosed space.

Through the haze of dust and disarray, she appeared. The porcelain mask gleamed sickly in the fractured light, its cracks warping her smile into something truly macabre. Mimi's movements were unnatural, her body contorting grotesquely as she surged towards Nichols.

The gleam of a blade—or was it something even worse?—flashed in her hand. Nichols reacted just in time, his wrench meeting her strike with a clang that resonated down the corridor.

"Get back!" Nichols commanded, muscles bulging as he parried Mimi's relentless assault.

Tadd remained paralyzed, the crowbar in his hands feeling absurdly inadequate. His heart pounded ferociously, terror rooting him to the spot as he watched the horrifying tableau unfold before him. The nightmare was real, and it was relentless.

Tadd's legs felt like they were dissolving into nothing as he watched Dee's desperate assault. The hammer swung in a wild, uncontrolled arc, cutting through the air where Mimi had been moments before. She evaded with a fluid, smoke-like twist, her cackling laughter scraping against Tadd's nerves.

"Stay still, you psychotic—" Dee's curse was abruptly severed as Mimi retreated with disjointed, almost puppet-like jerks. Her movements were uncannily wrong, sending shivers down Tadd's spine.

Nichols lunged next, his wrench aimed with desperate precision. It connected, sending a reverberating clang through the air and spiderwebbing a crack across the mask's porcelain surface. Mimi responded with another round of that eerie, bone-chilling laughter, tilting her head at an angle that defied anatomy, the grotesque smile of her mask a mockery of their efforts.

The crowbar slipped in Tadd's sweat-slicked grip, his heartbeat thundering so loudly in his ears it nearly drowned out the chaos. This nightmare was unreal, beyond comprehension. The metal bar felt absurdly ineffective, a child's toy against a nightmarish reality.

"Fuck this!" Tadd blurted out, terror overriding reason. Instinctively, his feet propelled him backward, away from the unfolding horror. He turned and fled, the hallway morphing into a dark, endless tunnel as he ran, his flashlight beam jerking frantically against the walls, throwing monstrous shadows.

Behind him, the sounds of chaos splintered in diffcrent directions—Dee and Nichols dividing their efforts. Whether it was strategic or foolish, Tadd couldn't determine; his mind was too clouded by fear. His lungs burned with the effort of his flight, his route dictated by panic as he navigated the mansion's labyrinthine corridors.

The sounds of pursuit echoed, distorted by the hall's acoustics, making it impossible to discern their origin. His panicked escape led him around a blind corner and—

A dead end. A wall loomed up, stark and unyielding. No doors, no windows, no escape. Tadd spun around, the crowbar raised defensively, his whole body tensed for a confrontation.

The footsteps intensified, then faded, moving off down another corridor, leaving Tadd isolated in his terror. Silence fell like a heavy shroud, punctuated only by his own heavy breathing and the loud pounding of his heart. Alone in the oppressive darkness, Tadd clutched the crowbar, waiting for what might come next, every sense alert.

Tadd's legs shook uncontrollably as he pressed himself against the wall, his heart pounding with such ferocity he feared it might burst through his chest. The crowbar felt like dead weight in his trembling hand, his grip loosening from sheer exhaustion and terror. Sweat trickled into his eyes, stinging and blurring his vision, but he was too petrified to wipe it away.

The oppressive silence was punctuated only by his own ragged breaths, each inhale sharp and desperate. His mind was a whirlwind of horrific images: Josh's grotesquely disfigured body, Mimi's eerie, fluid movements, that hauntingly cracked porcelain mask catching the light of their flashlights. He had always fashioned himself as tough, a facade now crumbling under the weight of his raw fear.

A floorboard groaned with menace in the darkness.

"Dee?" His voice barely rose above a whisper, laden with vulnerability. "Nichols?"

No answer came, only the thick, suffocating silence returning to envelop him.

The darkness felt alive, a tangible force encircling him, heavy with the stench of decay that invaded his nostrils and clawed at his throat, urging him to gag. His flashlight sliced through the gloom, the beam illuminating patches of peeling wallpaper and the rotten carcasses of floorboards beneath his feet.

Then, a sound—a melody so faint it was almost lost within the stillness—a lullaby distorted and perverted, hummed by something that had long ago shed any semblance of humanity.

Tadd's blood chilled in his veins as the tune crawled under his skin. His hand trembled violently as he swept the flashlight down the corridor. There, at the far end, a glimpse of white—a bloodstained gown that vanished around a corner with the swiftness of a specter.

"No, no, no," he murmured, his back pressing harder against the cold, unyielding wall.

The lullaby intensified, morphing into a chilling giggle that bounced eerily off the walls, envcloping him in a cacophony of madness. The sound was omnipresent, a suffocating echo in the confined space.

The flashlight slipped from his weak grasp and crashed to the floor. It spun out of control, casting wildly gyrating shadows that danced across the walls like malevolent spirits reveling in his dread.

The laughter escalated into a frenzied cackle, piercing and near, growing ever closer.

Tadd's strength deserted him; his legs buckled, and he slid to the floor, each breath a gasp of sheer terror. The erratic beam of his flashlight captured a figure approaching—a jerky, unnatural gait that spoke of marionette limbs pulled by unseen strings. As the light flickered across the corridor, it illuminated the cracked porcelain mask emerging from the shadows, its grotesque smile a harbinger of unspeakable horrors yet to come.

Screams from the Hollow

T add's back slammed against the crumbling wall as the ghastly figure of Mimi, donning the cracked porcelain mask, slithered out from the shadows. His hand quivered uncontrollably as he fumbled to switch on his phone's flashlight, the feeble beam doing little to combat the suffocating darkness enveloping him. The crowbar in his other hand felt absurdly ineffectual, more like a child's toy than a weapon against the nightmare unfurling before him.

"Stay the fuck back!" The intensity of his own voice startled him as it cracked through the silence, echoing off the dilapidated walls and warped floorboards of the hallway. The words returned to him distorted, as if the mansion itself mocked his feeble attempt at bravery. "I mean it! I'll bash your fucking head in!"

The threat tasted hollow, bitter with the tang of his palpable fear. His knees buckled slightly as Mimi took another disjointed step forward, her movements grotesquely unnatural. The mask caught the tremulous light, casting eerie shadows that seemed to animate the ghoulish smile etched upon it—a smile that seemed to promise tortures far worse than death.

Then, just audible over the pounding of his own heart, a lullaby began to hum—a sound so twisted and broken it made his skin prickle with dread. Mimi's head cocked to an impossible angle, the haunting melody growing louder as she drew nearer, her presence oppressive and terrifying.

"No, no, no..." Tadd's voice was a desperate whisper, his fear escalating into sheer panic. In a last-ditch, frantic effort, he threw his phone at her. It clattered against the wall, its light flickering out as he seized the moment to dart past her, the darkness swiftly reclaiming the space.

He plunged into the pitch-black corridor, his lungs burning as he gasped for air. Each labored breath sounded like a thunderclap in his ears. The crowbar swung wildly at his side, thudding against his leg with each frenzied step. He sprinted, the decrepit floorboards groaning unnervingly underfoot, threatening to splinter and collapse beneath his weight, as he raced to escape the horrifying melody that seemed to chase after him, echoing through the halls of the cursed mansion.

Tadd lurched through the pitch-black corridor, his heart thundering like a drum inside his chest. The crowbar in his hand was slick with sweat, making it difficult to maintain a firm grip. He collided with a wall, the impact sending a jolt of pain through his shoulder as he fumbled desperately along its surface. His fingers traced the peeling wallpaper, clawing for something, anything, that might offer an escape.

Behind him, the sound of Mimi's footsteps echoed through the corridor, their deliberate pace chillingly unhurried. The distorted strains of that haunting lullaby wound its way through the darkness, each note sharper, closer, tightening the noose of dread around his neck. His breathing was sharp and erratic, each gasp a knife edge of panic slicing through the suffocating fear.

His hands, shaking uncontrollably, finally closed around the cold metal of a doorknob. With no time to think, driven by raw instinct, he wrenched the door open and threw himself into the relative safety of what appeared to be a closet. The door snapped shut behind him with a soft click that, in the oppressive silence of his hiding place, sounded like a gunshot.

The closet was a tomb of forgotten things. The musty scent of decay was overpowering, and unidentified fabrics brushed against his face—old coats or dresses, abandoned to the embrace of time. Dust particles flirted with his nostrils, threatening an ill-timed sneeze. He pressed his back against the wall, trying to dissolve into the shadows, to become

nothing more than a part of the cramped, forgotten spa
ce.

Outside, Mimi's footsteps came to a haunting halt right by the door. Tadd's hands flew to his mouth, pressing hard against his lips to stifle his breaths, which threatened to burst forth in loud, revealing gasps. Sweat cascaded down his back, each drop a cold trail of terror.

The doorknob twitched slightly, a subtle, terrifying gesture as if testing the door. The faint scrape of metal against wood was almost inaudible, yet to Tadd, it was a clarion call of impending doom. The handle went still again, a moment suspended in time, heavy with the threat of discovery.

Tadd's legs trembled, his entire body poised on the edge of collapse as he waited in the choking darkness, each second stretching into eternity. He prayed silently, fervently, that she would move on, that the door would remain closed, that he would remain unseen in the dark embrace of the closet.

The oppressive silence clung to Tadd like a second skin, his nerves stretched taut as the edge of a razor. His hands shook visibly around the crowbar's icy metal, sweat coursing down his spine despite the chilling darkness enveloping him in the closet. Each breath felt labored, the musty air thick with decay and the ghost of his own fear.

From somewhere down the hall, a faint giggle sliced through the tense quiet—distant enough to whisper hope yet near enough to send a spike of fresh terror piercing through his core. Flashes of Josh's brutalized body, and the haunting visage of that twisted porcelain smile, surged through his mind. The crowbar in his grip seemed laughably inadequate against the nightmares made flesh that stalked them.

"Fuck this," he murmured, the words a mere thread of sound, yet they sparked a defiant surge within him, an adrenaline-fueled realization. Staying hidden in this closet would seal his fate, trapping him like a rat in a cage. Running might offer a sliver of a chance.

A sliver of moonlight seeped through a distant window, casting a weak lifeline of light that was barely enough to navigate by. Clutching the crowbar until his knuckles whitened with the effort, Tadd took a deep breath, then another. On the third, he flung the door open with a force borne of desperation and swung the crowbar through the air in a wild, sweeping arc.

The hallway lay barren before him, shrouded in shadows that pooled in every crevice like dark, ominous pools of ink. No sign of Mimi, no glimpse of the cracked mask or those vacant, soulless eyes. Without a moment's hesitation, Tadd sprinted towards the feeble moonlight, his footsteps echoing loudly on the uneven, groaning floorboards.

"Dee! Nichols!" His voice shattered the haunting silence, high-pitched with stark desperation. "Where the fuck are you guys?"

As he ran, the shadows around him seemed to animate, twisting and writhing at the periphery of his vision, as if they were alive and reaching for him. Suddenly, his foot snagged on a protruding board, hurling him forward with merciless force. He hit the ground hard, the breath whooshing out of him in a painful gasp, his world reduced to the sharp, immediate pain of impact. The crowbar clattered from his grasp, skidding away into the consuming darkness, its sound mocking his plight as it faded into silence.

Pain radiated through Tadd's chest like a wildfire as he gasped for breath, the oppressive darkness around him suffocating in its totality. His hands, trembling and slick with sweat, scraped against the splintered wood of the floorboards as he struggled to rise, each attempt racking his bruised ribs with fresh agony.

A sinister scraping halted his movements—metal dragging along wood, slow and menacing. The sound approached from behind, accompanied by the sinister rustle of fabric. Tadd's heart pounded violently against his ribcage, the chill of fear sending cold sweat down his back.

"Hide and seek is over." The voice, chillingly child-like and unnaturally cheerful, floated through the darkness. "Time to play a new game."

A scream ripped from Tadd's throat as icy fingers clamped around his ankle. Desperation surged through him; he kicked out frantically, his heel striking something unyielding, but the grip on his leg only tightened. His fingernails tore against the rough wood, splintering painfully as Mimi dragged him back down the pitch-black corridor.

"No, please!" His voice was a choked cry, a raw, desperate plea as he thrashed against her iron hold. "Someone help me!"

Dim moonlight spilled through a distant window, casting a weak glow that just outlined the menacing silhouette looming over him. The cracked porcelain mask caught the faint light, eerily gleaming as Mimi raised his own crowbar above her head. The metal glinted dully, a grim harbinger of the pain to come.

Tadd raised his arms, a pitiful shield against the inevitable. The crowbar cut through the air, a silent promise of agony. An excruciating blaze of pain seared his back as the crowbar smashed down, tearing through muscle and bone with brutal force. His scream was a grotesque gurgle, blood bubbling up and choking him.

The sound of his spine snapping was a gruesome echo in the desolate hallway, each breath now a torturous effort as his crushed lungs fought for air. Blood warmed his back, soaking his shirt and spreading beneath him, staining the ancient wood.

Mimi wrenched the crowbar free with a sickening squelch that made Tadd's stomach churn. He attempted a crawl, a pathetic, scrambling effort, but his legs were unresponsive, dead weights. Panic surged as the horrifying truth set in—his body was broken, paralyzed.

Mimi crouched close, her mask inches from his face, tilting her head in that horrifyingly curious angle. "Shhh," she whispered, a perverse gentleness in her voice as if she were comforting him. "The pain won't last much longer."

With a swift, cruel motion, she drove the crowbar through Tadd's open mouth, smashing it deep into the floorboards beneath. The impact shattered his teeth, sending splinters of bone and sprays of blood arcing across the floor as the metal pinned him mercilessly in place. His body convulsed once, a final involuntary spasm, before falling eerily still, his eyes fixed in a vacant, horrified stare.

Jess's flashlight beam sliced through the darkness, the narrow light illuminating the blood-spattered hallway that stretched menacingly before them. Her heart hammered in her chest, each beat a loud echo in her own ears as she led the group forward. The floorboards creaked underfoot, their warped surfaces groaning with each step, while the stench of blood—metallic and overpowering—mingled with the dank, musty air of the mansion.

"Tadd?" Nichols's voice rang out from behind her, tight with tension and thinly controlled panic. "Where the fuck are you?"

A shape materialized from the shadows ahead—a figure crumpled on the floor. Jess's breath hitched, her throat constricting as her flashlight revealed

Tadd's body, grotesquely twisted and broken. The crowbar protruded from his mouth, a horrific metal tongue, pinning him to the blood-soaked wood. His eyes, wide and glassy, stared vacantly at the ceiling, capturing his last moment of terror.

Jess's hand clapped over her mouth, nausea surging as her stomach churned violently. The flashlight in her trembling hand cast eerie, dancing shadows over the gruesome tableau. Just above Tadd's corpse, the wall was defiled with a child's crude drawing—a stick-figure house sketched in his blood. Next to it, the name "Mimi" was scrawled in jagged, dripping crimson letters across the faded wallpaper.

"Oh god," Jess gasped, her voice a choked whisper as she fought to suppress a sob that clawed its way up her throat. Her fingers pressed against her lips, desperately trying to stifle the scream that threatened to burst forth.

Nichols moved closer, his boots squelching in the expanding pool of blood. "Jesus Christ," he murmured, the raw shock in his voice hollowing out his usual authoritative tone.

Behind them, Micah doubled over, the sound of her retching resonating in the silent hallway, interspersed with her quiet, desperate sobs. Jaime reached out, steadying her with a firm grip on her shoulder as Micah's stomach emptied onto the dusty floor.

Dee stood motionless, his hammer dangling uselessly by his side. "We're fucked," he murmured, his voice barely audible, laden with dread. "We're so fucking fucked."

Jess's gaze remained locked on Tadd's disfigured face, the brutality of his end laid bare in the harsh beam of her light. Just hours earlier, he had been alive, filled with laughter and idle jokes. Now, he was reduced to a mere object in their nightmarish reality.

Silence enveloped the group, heavy and suffocating, as the gravity of their predicament descended upon them. The oppressive darkness of the mansion seemed to close in, tightening around them like a vise.

Nichols shifted, the sound of his wrench scraping against the floor as he adjusted his stance. "We need to—" His voice broke, the strain evident. He cleared his throat, attempting to regain some semblance of control. "We need to keep moving."

Yet, they remained frozen, transfixed by the horror of their fallen friend and the chilling artwork that announced the presence of their tormentor.

Jess's flashlight flickered momentarily, the light dimming before it stabilized, casting long shadows across the corridor. In that brief lapse into darkness, a faint, childlike giggle seemed to drift down the hallway, its eerie sound mingling with the cold air, reminding them that Mimi was still there, somewhere in the dark, waiting.

TRAILS STAINED RED

Jess's legs felt like they were mired in sludge, each step a monumental effort as she dragged her gaze away from the macabre tableau of Tadd's mutilated corpse. Forcing herself to lead the group deeper into the mansion, her flashlight beam sliced through the enveloping darkness, revealing the pervasive decay that seemed to spread like a living entity before them.

The walls themselves appeared to be succumbing to the rot, the wallpaper bubbling and peeling away as if in revulsion. A thick, sour stench assaulted her nostrils—blood intermingled with the dank mildew of decay and another scent, something foul that twisted her stomach into knots. The floorboards moaned under their weight, each creak amplified to a groan in the suffocating silence that cloaked them.

"Wait," whispered Micah, her voice struggling to pierce the oppressive atmosphere. She pointed to the floor where a dark smear marred the wood, trailing away into the shadows. "Is that... is that blood?"

Jess's throat constricted as her flashlight followed the chilling trail. The blood shone with a wet sheen, unsettlingly fresh. Her fingers shook as she tightened her grip on the flashlight, the beam trembling across the gruesome path.

"Holy shit," Jaime gasped, her usual composure splintered by fear. Jess swung her light to where Jaime's own beam spotlighted the wall ahead. There, scrawled in blood still slick and dripping, were crude, jagged letters that mocked their plight.

Dee stepped forward, his posture tense, the hammer in his hand a small comfort against the horror they faced. The fresh blood dripped slowly down the wall, drawn into ghastly rivulets by gravity, its bright redness a stark contrast against the peeling, faded wallpaper.

Nichols's hand reached out, his touch cautious as he pulled Jaime slightly back from the disturbing message. It was a protective gesture, tinged with a vulnerability that Jess hadn't seen in him before. His face was etched with lines of fear, mirroring the dread that gnawed relentlessly at Jess's insides.

As they stood in the dim corridor, surrounded by the evidence of the nightmare that hunted them, the air between them thickened with unspoken terror. The stark reality of their situation was etched in every shadow, every whisper of movement that the light touched. In the mansion's heart, where even the walls seemed to bleed, their chances of survival dimmed like the faltering beam of Jess's flashlight.

Jess's flashlight beam traced the path of a sinister blood trail as it snaked around a corner, vanishing into a side room. Her heart thudded against her ribs, the rapid beats resonating in her ears as the metallic scent of blood intensified, drying her mouth with fear.

"Stay close," she murmured, her voice a whisper lost in the vast silence of the mansion. It was unclear if she was comforting her companions or herself. The floorboards beneath their feet groaned in protest as they edged forward, the weight of their collective dread heavy in the air.

The door to the side room was barely hanging on its rusted hinges. Jess's hand trembled visibly as she nudged it open further; the sharp creak of the hinges set her teeth on edge. Her flashlight cut a swath through the engulfing darkness, revealing a scene of chaos—broken furniture and shattered glass strewn about the floor until the beam halted abruptly.

A choked scream strangled itself in her throat.

Katie's body was propped grotesquely against the far wall, her once pristine designer suit now marred by a gruesome tapestry of crimson. Deep, savage gouges defaced her face, her flesh hanging in tatters, the handiwork of an unspeakable violence. Her throat was slashed open, a horrific mimicry of a smile, with blood still seeping from the ghastly wound. Her eyes, once lively and assertive, now stared blankly into oblivion, devoid of any spark.

"Oh god." The words escaped Jess's lips as she recoiled, a surge of bile rising to her throat. The trembling beam of her flashlight lingered morbidly on Katie's corpse, uncovering more chilling details—the broken fingernails, the defensive wounds that marred her arms, the unnatural angle of her legs.

Micah moved past Jess, dropping to her knees with a thud beside Katie's body. Her hands hovered over the lifeless form, trembling uncontrollably. "She... she was just trying to sell this place. She didn't... she wasn't supposed to..." Her voice was punctuated by sharp, ragged breaths, each one laden with panic and despair.

The acrid taste of vomit threatened to overwhelm Jess as she turned away, pressing a fist tightly against her mouth as her stomach churned violently. The room seemed to spin around her, the pervasive stench of death assaulting her senses, pushing her to the brink.

"Son of a bitch," Nichols growled through gritted teeth, his voice laced with a restrained fury that cut through the thick, oppressive atmosphere of the room. "We need to get out of here. Now." His command, though desperate, was clear, an urgent call to action in the face of overwhelming horror.

A high-pitched giggle pierced the still air, reverberating off the crumbling walls of the mansion, ensnaring Jess and her companions in a chilling auditory maze. Jess's muscles tensed, her hands gripping the flashlight tighter as she swept the beam across the room, desperately searching for the source of that eerie sound. It wrapped around them like a macabre melody, crawling under her skin, making her flesh prickle with dread.

"Where the fuck is it coming from?" Jaime's voice cracked as she spun around, her own flashlight slicing through the darkness in frantic arcs. Her hysteria was palpable, a raw edge of panic. "I can't—I can't tell where—"

Dee's hand shot out, his grip firm as he caught Jaime's wrist, halting her chaotic movements. "Stop moving the light around like that. You're just making the shadows worse."

The giggle echoed again, unmistakably closer, threading through the tense air with malicious playfulness. Jess's heart thudded painfully against her ribs, the urge to flee, to escape this nightmare and run blindly through the mansion's dark, endless corridors nearly overwhelming her. Her throat felt tight, constricted with fear, as flashes of Katie's horrifically mutilated body invaded her mind.

"Everyone quiet," Nichols hissed, his voice a ghost of a whisper, hardly disturbing the heavy silence. "We need to move. The study's just down the hall—stay together, stay quiet."

Jess nodded, her breaths shallow and controlled as they edged forward. Each step was a calculated risk, the ancient floorboards groaning under their weight, threatening to scream their presence to the entire house. The darkness felt alive, encroaching on their fragile circle of light, and Jess was almost certain she saw shadows flitting just beyond its reach, watching, waiting.

They reached the study, its door ajar, groaning on its hinges as they eased inside. The room was a tomb of knowledge, dust motes swirling in their flashlight beams, the air thick with the musty scent of old books and forgotten secrets. Jess's light roved over the chaos of overturned furniture and scattered papers, finally settling on Micah, who stood frozen by a toppled bookshelf.

"Look at this." Micah's voice found strength as she pulled a rolled bundle of papers from beneath the debris, her hands steadying as she spread them across a nearby desk. The yellowed blueprints of the mansion unfurled under her trembling fingers. "These show all the original layouts—including some rooms that aren't on the regular floor plan."

Josh leaned in, his features drawn in concentration, his hand gesturing for Jess to hold the light steady. His eyes traced the lines of the blueprints, absorbing the intricate details, searching for something—anything—that might give them an edge, a way to understand the labyrinth they were trapped in. As he studied the faded drawings, a glimmer of something like determination—or perhaps desperation—flickered in his gaze.

Jess observed as Nichols's finger traced the faded lines of the blueprint, navigating a narrow passage hidden within the mansion's walls. His expression was intense, the set of his jaw tight as he delved into the architectural secrets sprawled before him.

"There," he said, his finger pausing at a confluence of lines. "Crawlspace behind the kitchen, leads into a network of service tunnels. Looks like the old own-ers had a whole system for staff to move unseen."

The blueprint rustled under his touch, the shad-owy flicker of their flashlights animating the ink lines, transforming them into squirming shadows on the yellowed paper. Jess's grip on her flashlight tightened, her pulse quickening at the thought of threading through those cramped, hidden channels.

Nichols lifted his gaze to meet hers, his eyes a mix of resolve and simmering anxiety. "It's tight. Very tight. But it might be our only chance to get out."

A chill draft sidled through the study, mingling the must of ancient books with the metallic taint of blood that still lingered in the air. Jess drew her jack-et tighter around her, a vain attempt to block out the cold that seemed to gnaw at her very marrow.

"You want us to crawl through the fucking walls?" Dee's tone was a blend of disbelief and anger, his hand white-knuckled around the hammer's handle. "After what happened to Josh? To Tadd?"

"We don't have a choice," Nichols responded, his voice low and firm as he rolled up the blueprint with precise, measured movements. "Front door's locked, windows are barred. It's this or nothing."

He left the sentence hanging, the unspoken words heavier than any they could dare to say aloud.

Micah pressed closer to Jess the blueprint clutched in her hand, her breathing shallow and rapid. Nearby, Jaime paced restlessly by the door, her usual confidence replaced by jittery agitation.

"Let's move," Nichols murmured, his whisper almost inaudible. "Quick and quiet. Like our lives depend on it."

Because indeed they did.

They exited the study in a single-file line, their flashlight beams slicing through the thick darkness. Each step they took echoed in the vast silence of the mansion, their cautious movements amplifying the oppressive stillness that enveloped them.

Jess trailed behind Nichols, her flashlight's beam flickering across the deteriorating elegance of peeling wallpaper and warped floorboards. Nichols paused intermittently to scrutinize their path, his jaw set firm with resolve. Jaime's footsteps echoed unevenly behind Jess, her presence a constant reminder of their dire circumstances.

"This is such bullshit," Jaime hissed under her breath, her voice threading through the dense air with barely suppressed panic. "We're going to die in here like fucking rats in a maze."

Jess's throat tightened, the words she wanted to offer caught in the vice of her own fear. Around them, the shadows seemed to throb with a malevolent life of their own, every creak and whisper of the old mansion amplifying the feeling of unseen eyes watching.

Bringing up the rear, Dee clutched his hammer, the metal head catching the dim light, casting ominous reflections. The memory of Tadd, armed yet helpless, haunted Jess, a stark reminder of their vulnerability.

As they rounded another corner, Nichols stopped abruptly, raising his hand for silence. "Should be here," he whispered, his voice no more than a breath as his fingers explored the wall. "Behind this panel."

Micah, her face a pale mask of anxiety under her flashlight's beam, stepped up to join him. The wall loomed featureless and unyielding before them, its surface marred only by the scars of decay and neglect, offering no hint of the secret passages outlined in their crumbling map.

"I don't see anything," Micah's voice wavered, her flashlight's beam trembling across the wall. "Are you sure this is—"

Their words shattered as a high, chilling laugh sliced through the corridor, a sharp echo that rebounded off the walls with a clarity that was almost tangible. The sound ensnared them, tightening like a noose, its icy grip paralyzing.

Jess whirled around, her movements frantic, as her hands, slick with cold sweat, struggled to maintain their grip on her flashlight. For a fleeting moment, the beam cut through the darkness and caught the horrifying sight of that cracked porcelain mask. The mask's twisted smile and empty eye sockets were a grotesque mockery of human expression, a visage of nightmare etched into the gloom.

Then, with a sputter of betrayal, her flashlight flickered out, enveloping them in an oppressive blackness that seemed to swallow every shred of hope.

Broken Trust

J ess's palm slammed against the dead flashlight, desperation clawing at her throat as the stale, metallic tang of blood permeated the air. The unnervingly close sound of Mimi's ragged breathing grazed her neck, sending shivers down her spine. Her fingers quaked as she struck the flashlight once more, a desperate plea for light in the enveloping darkness.

Suddenly, multiple beams sprang to life, slicing through the gloom and catching Mimi's grotesque porcelain mask in their unforgiving glare. The cracked surface of the mask fractured the light into a blinding kaleidoscope, eliciting an unearthly shriek from behind it.

"Move!" Nichols's command cut sharply through the chaos, urgent and commanding.

Propelled by fear and adrenaline, Jess surged forward, brushing past the recoiling figure of Mimi.

The others pounded behind her, their hurried steps thundering against the decayed wood of the mansion's floors. The corridor seemed to constrict around them, its shadows contorting wildly in the erratic dance of their flashlight beams.

A sudden crash whipped Jess's head around. Micah was sprawled on the floor, entangled in the remains of a shattered chair. Jaime tripped over her, tumbling to the ground with a curse.

"Fuck!" Jaime's scream sliced through the air as Mimi's ghastly pale hand reached out from the shadows, her fingers skimming Jaime's ankle.

Dee's figure blurred into motion as he pulled Jaime from the brink of Mimi's grasp, while Nichols hoisted Micah back to her feet with hurried strength. They continued their frenetic dash down the corridor, the haunting echo of Mimi's laughter chasing them like a malevolent specter.

Ahead, Jess spotted salvation—a door. She threw her weight against it, the old wood groaning under the force before relenting. They tumbled into a cramped space, the door slamming shut behind them with a cloud of dust rising in protest. The weak glow of their surviving flashlights revealed a room imprisoned by time—peeling wallpaper and shattered remnants of furniture.

"We can't keep running like this," Jess declared, her voice laced with fatigue and frustration as she switched on her cell phone's light. She gasped for air, her breaths heavy, tasting the coppery dust that filled the room.

Nichols slumped against the wall, his wrench dangling from one hand, his face glistening with sweat under the dim illumination.

On the far side of the room, Jaime's eyes seared into Micah with raw, unmasked fury. "You almost got me killed, you clumsy bitch," she spat, her words dripping with venom and echoing with a foreboding tone in the cramped quarters.

Micah cowered against the cold, unforgiving wall, her posture shrinking as Jaime's fury advanced like a storm. Jess's body coiled instinctively, ready to intervene before blows could fly.

"I-I didn't mean to—" Micah's voice fractured under the strain, a fragile whisper in the oppressive darkness.

"You didn't mean to?" Jaime's accusation cut deep, her finger thrusting accusingly at Micah's chest. "That psycho bitch almost grabbed me because you're stumbling around like a fool. Two of us are already dead because of this mess, and you nearly added me to that list!"

The sound of blood roaring in Jess's ears underscored the gravity of the confrontation as she watched the despair wash over Micah's face. The young woman drew her arms tightly around herself, her breaths sharp and ragged, eyes glistening with tears.

"I'm sorry," Micah murmured, the tears breaking free and tracing clear paths down her dirt-smudged face. "I just tripped over the chair... I didn't see it, it was so dark. Please—"

"Sorry doesn't bring Josh or Tadd back," Jaime's voice escalated, slicing through the thick air with its sharpness. "And it sure as hell won't save us when that masked freak comes for the rest of us one by one—"

Dee interposed his solid frame between the quarreling women, his presence like a barricade. The hammer by his side seemed almost superfluous to the implicit threat his stature posed.

"Back off," he growled, the warning clear in his tone aimed at Jaime.

Jaime scoffed, her arms folding defiantly. "Sure, take her side. Always protecting the weak link, huh?"

"Enough." The command came from Nichols, resolute and cold as steel. He detached himself from the shadowed wall, his wrench gleaming dimly in the scant light. "This stops now. If we turn on each other, we're as good as dead. That's the end of it."

Each word Nichols spoke seemed to hang in the dank air, a stern reminder of their dire circumstances. The group's fragile cohesion hung by a thread, frayed by fear and suspicion, yet held from snapping by the sheer necessity of survival.

Jess's heart thundered, a fierce drum against her chest, as she watched her group splinter under the strain. Fear left a metallic tang on her tongue, blending seamlessly with the air's decay.

"Stop it, all of you." Her voice cracked, worn thin by exertion and terror. "This is exactly what she wants. We're breaking down, making it easier for her to pick us off one by one." She swept her gaze across Jaime's scornful face to Micah's tear-streaked cheeks. "Turning on each other won't keep us alive."

Jaime's eyes rolled dismissively, her scoff slicing through the thick tension. "Save the kumbaya bullshit, Jess."

"What have you done?" Micah's voice, usually so quiet, sliced with unexpected sharpness into the fraught silence. "Besides complain? At least I'm trying to do something."

The words hung heavy in the stale air, a palpable beat before Jaime's face twisted with fury. She surged forward, fingers hooked like talons. Micah's back slammed against the wall as she tried to fend off the attack.

"Get off me!" Micah's scream reverberated off the walls, her arms flailing.

Nichols reacted swiftly, his large frame forcing itself between the clashing women. His wrench hit the floor with a heavy clang as he separated them. Micah staggered back, her breath ragged, her eyes burning holes into Jaime.

"I hope you die," she hissed, venom saturating her trembling whisper.

Dee's throaty clearing cut through the thickening air, drawing Jess's wary gaze. His dark eyes flickered from Nichols to her, heavy with unspoken words. "Jaime's right, though. We're just dragging dead weight."

Jess's heart sank. Not Dee. Not now.

He shrugged, his hammer swaying menacingly at his side. "Someone had to say it."

"You son of a bitch." Nichols's voice boomed as he snatched up his wrench, stepping toward Dee with thunderous intent. "The only reason you're backing her is you've been wanting to fuck her since we got here."

Dee's expression darkened, his stance hardening as he lifted his hammer defensively. "Watch your fucking mouth."

The two men faced off, each silhouette etched sharply against the flickering light, their shadows grotesque caricatures on the crumbling walls. Jess's stomach twisted into knots, witnessing the shadows dance a prelude to the violence brewing in the dimly lit corridor.

Jess's heart pounded furiously, echoing the betrayal flashing across her features as Jaime's fingers tightened around Dee's brawny forearm. A chilling smile played on Jaime's lips, her gaze piercing as she leaned into Dee.

"We're better off without them," Jaime whispered, her voice laced with malice, her eyes never leaving Dee's hardened face.

Dee's stern expression softened slightly under the influence of her touch. He nodded slowly, his hammer dropping to his side, his stance relaxing. He made his way to the door, the old floorboards groaning under his weight with every step.

Blood thundered in Jess's ears as she darted in front of them, her arms outstretched in a desperate attempt to barricade the doorway.

"Please," she implored, her voice trembling, breaking under the weight of her plea. "Don't do this. We need to stay together." The words felt hollow, bitter in her dry mouth.

Jaime's scoff sliced through the tense air, sharp and scornful. She pushed past Jess with deliberate force, her shoulder slamming into Jess, sending her reeling back. The breath whooshed from Jess's lungs as she staggered.

The door creaked with a foreboding sound as Dee pulled it open, revealing the dark, insatiable abyss beyond. Without a glance back, they stepped into the enveloping shadows, their footsteps a fading echo into nothingness.

The room expanded around Jess, the silence and darkness closing in, making the walls seem to draw nearer. She hugged herself tightly, trying to quell the shiver that ran through her.

She turned to see Nichols, his face a mask of fury, the muscles in his jaw working furiously. The wrench in his hand trembled with the intensity of his grip.

"What do we do now?" Jess's voice was barely audible, frail against the crushing silence.

Micah collapsed against the wall, sliding down to the floor with a hollow thud. Her gaze was lost, haunted. "They're not going to make it," she said softly, more to herself than to anyone else.

Nichols spat bitterly on the floor, his words harsh and unforgiving. "Fuck them. If they die, they die." His voice was devoid of sympathy, a stark declaration in the dark, stifling air.

Dee's grip on the hammer felt like his only tie to reality as they ventured deeper into the mansion's claustrophobic corridors. His flashlight beam struggled against the oppressive darkness, revealing only faint glimpses of the peeling wallpaper and rotting floorboards that sprawled before them. His heart thudded violently, a relentless drumbeat in his chest, yet he maintained a facade of calm for Jaime's sake.

"Keep moving," he murmured, his voice a low rasp in the thick air. "We gotta find a way out of this hellhole."

Jaime trailed him closely, her steps hesitant on the unstable wood. The mansion's stale air clung to the back of his throat, tasting of decay and the bitter tang of fear. Splitting from the group weighed heavily on him, but the need to act, to escape, had driven him forward.

Then, slicing through the silence, a high-pitched giggle resonated off the walls, chilling Dee's blood. It echoed ominously, playing tricks on their senses, a spectral sound that seemed to mock their plight.

"Do you hear that?" Jaime's voice broke, laced with unmistakable fear.

Dee tightened his hold on the hammer, his only anchor in the creeping dread. The weight of it in his hand was reassuring but utterly insufficient against the unknown horrors lurking in the shadows. He instinctively stepped closer to Jaime, a protective gesture as much for his reassurance as for hers.

"Stay close," he managed, his voice betraying a tremor he hadn't intended.

Their flashlights swept the crumbling interior, throwing monstrous shadows against the walls that twisted and moved as though alive. Suddenly, a shape flickered at the edge of his light—a brief, distorted silhouette that skittered across the wall, grotesque and fluid.

"Fuck," Jaime gasped, her voice quaking. "Dee..."

Positioning himself squarely between Jaime and the unknown, Dee scanned the hallway with sharp, darting glances, each shadow and sound magnifying his fear. His pulse hammered in his ears, mingling with the drip of distant, unseen water, or perhaps something far worse. The shadows seemed to pulse, infused with a malevolent presence.

"I don't like this," he whispered, the weight of the darkness pressing down on them. "Something's very wrong here."

Dee felt his blood freeze as a child's sing-song voice cut through the darkness, taunting, "Come play with me..." The voice echoed off the mansion's dilapidated walls, creating a disorienting cacophony that made it impossible to discern its origin. His flashlight swept through the corridor, illuminating nothing but the mansion's decaying innards—peeling wallpaper and rotting wood that seemed to absorb the light.

"She's fucking with us," Jaime whispered intensely, spinning around, her own flashlight beam creating wild, dancing shadows on the crumbling walls.

Gripping her arm firmly, Dee steadied her. "We need to move. Now!"

They dashed down the hallway, their footsteps heavy on the warped floorboards, the sound echoing back at them as if they were being chased by an unseen horde. Dee's heart hammered in his chest, adrenaline coursing through his veins as he tugged Jaime along.

The child's giggling chased them, a sound both close and far, growing increasingly manic. As they ran, Dee's flashlight beam jerked wildly, throwing grotesque shadows onto the walls that seemed to stretch out towards them like the fingers of the damned. The air thickened, filling with the taste of copper and decay, pressing against them with the weight of the grave.

"Faster," Dee panted, his voice strained to breaking. The hammer in his hand was slick with his sweat, its weight a grim reminder of the danger they faced.

Rounding a corner, they skidded to a stop before a barricade of debris. Collapsed beams and broken ceiling fragments blocked their path, the rotten wood testament to years of neglect. "No, no, no," Jaime moaned, her voice a whisper of despair as she pressed back against Dee.

From behind them, the sound of footsteps approached, slow and deliberate, accompanied by that haunting, childlike humming. Dee positioned himself protectively in front of Jaime, his muscles tensed for a fight. He raised his hammer, his other hand clutching the flashlight, which now revealed a chilling sight: a cracked porcelain mask, its eerie smile mocking them from the shadows.

Mimi emerged from the darkness, her tattered dress swaying with each step, the giggle morphing into a full-throated laugh behind the grotesque mask.

Jaime's scream tore through the silence of the mansion, a sound so filled with terror it seemed to multiply, echoing off the walls and filling the space until it felt as though the entire mansion screamed with her.

Death's Embrace

Mimi advanced, her porcelain mask gleaming dimly as it caught the sparse light filtering through the boarded-up hallway window. Dee's muscles coiled tight, and he swung the hammer with all his might. The head struck her shoulder, a solid, resounding thud vibrating up his arms. Mimi recoiled, her tattered dress fluttering around her like dead leaves caught in a violent gust.

But the flicker of triumph in Dee's eyes extinguished as quickly as it had ignited. Mimi recovered with a supernatural swiftness, her countermove fluid and predatory. Amid the frenetic scramble, the hammer slipped from Dee's slick grip, clattering across the decaying wood beneath them.

His heart stalled when Mimi's icy fingers clamped around his throat. The mask hovered mere inches from his face, its eerie, painted smile taunting him.

Through the empty eye holes, he saw not eyes, but the abyss of something profoundly inhuman.

Jaime's hurried steps were a distant sound until she materialized with the lost hammer in hand. With a desperate, arcing swing, she struck Mimi on the back of the head. A gruesome crack resonated through the stale air of the hallway.

"Move!" Dee's voice tore from his throat, ragged and urgent.

Mimi's grip slackened, a guttural hiss—a sound more beast than human—escaping her as she staggered back.

Seizing the moment, Dee grasped Jaime's hand, pulling her along as they dashed down the corridor, the decrepit wallpaper blurring past. Mimi's heavy footsteps echoed behind them, a relentless pursuit that seemed to quicken.

Suddenly, the dreadful pounding of her steps halted.

Dee and Jaime came to a sharp stop, their breathing harsh in the unnerving quiet. Sweat beaded Dee's forehead, dripping down as he listened intently for any hint of Mimi's position.

"Why did she stop?" Jaime's whisper just reached Dee's ears, her voice quivering with unmasked terror. Her grip tightened on his arm, her nails digging into his flesh.

"She's playing with us," Dee murmured back, his hold on the hammer firm despite the shaking of his hands. The familiar heft of the weapon did little to assuage his fear, a stark reminder of the dire reality they faced in the encroaching shadows.

In the dimly lit room, Dee jammed a chair under the door handle while Jaime dragged a dusty dresser to reinforce their makeshift barricade. The scrape of wood against the creaky floorboards shattered the oppressive silence. "This will hold, right?" Jaime's voice cracked, tinged with panic.

Dee nodded, though his eyes continued to scour the room for anything else that might fortify their sanctuary. The feeble beams of their flashlights cast ghostly shadows against the peeling wallpaper and tattered curtains, painting everything with a hint of desolation. The air was thick with the must of decay, like a library forgotten by time.

Jaime sat heavily on the edge of the crumbling bed, her flashlight trembling in her grip, casting erratic shadows that danced like specters across the walls. Dee knelt before her, his rough hands steadying hers, his voice a low, calming presence. "It should hold until daylight. We'll have a better chance to find a way out then." He glanced toward the window, its grimy panes barely offering a view of the moonlit grounds outside, transforming the familiar into something alien.

Catching her breath, Jaime's gaze met his, her eyes swimming with fear and a desperate kind of daring. "So, you want to fuck me?" Her voice was rough, not just from the terror, but from the edge of something else, something fiercely alive beneath the fear.

Dee's answer was lost as Jaime reached out, her fingers tangling in his shirt, pulling him close with a reckless sort of urgency. Their lips met in a hard, desperate kiss, a collision of fear, defiance, and raw need. They clung to each other, not just for warmth but as if bracing against the storm of horrors outside.

Clothes were shed not with passion but with a frantic urgency to feel alive, to affirm life amidst the encroaching shadows of death. Their bodies came together with a rough, almost savage intensity, each movement a rebellion against the night's terror. Jaime's breaths were ragged against Dee's ear, her whispers a litany against the darkness.

As they moved together, the room around them faded, reduced to nothing but the urgent heat of their intertwined forms. The world narrowed to the sound of their quickened breaths and the soft creak of the aged bed under their weight. In this bubble of flickering light and shadow, the horror outside was held at bay, if only for a moment.

Their climax was sharp, almost brutal in its intensity, a peak that shattered the mounting tension, leaving them gasping, a tangle of limbs and damp skin in the aftermath. They lay together in the aftermath, the silence not empty but full of their shared ragged breaths.

In the fragile quiet after, Dee's arm remained wrapped protectively around Jaime, their bodies a barrier against the night's chill. Outside, the mansion creaked and settled, a reminder of the nightmare that still waited beyond their fragile sanctuary. In this fleeting sanctuary, they found not peace, but a momentary reprieve, a breath caught between the beats of a terror-stricken heart.

Dee's pulse thundered in his ears as he yanked his jeans back on, hands still trembling from the raw urgency of their encounter. The hammer lay nearby on the nightstand, its metal head reflecting the scant moonlight filtering through the filthy window. Behind him, the sound of Jaime's hurried movements as she fumbled with her clothing filled the suffocating silence of the room.

Suddenly, a high-pitched giggle sliced through the quiet, chilling Dee to his core. His fingers instinctively closed around the hammer's solid grip as the sinister laughter echoed again, now unmistakably closer, underscored by the sinister scrape of something sharp dragging across wood.

"No..." he whispered, his voice a hoarse thread of sound. His eyes darted around, scanning the shadows that seemed to creep and curl around the edges of the weak light. Moonlight warped across the walls, transforming benign shadows into menacing figures.

"She's here," Jaime's whisper just reached him, laden with a terror that mirrored his own.

The room's air thickened as that giggle twisted into a grotesque, gurgling mockery, and the scraping intensified—slow, deliberate, like the sound of nails clawing at the inside of the walls. Dee felt a cold sweat break out along his spine as he positioned himself protectively in front of Jaime, his hands white-knuckled around the hammer's handle. The familiar weight of the tool did little to comfort him against the palpable dread that filled the room.

"Get ready to run," he hissed without looking back, nodding toward the door they had barricaded with a dresser. His gaze remained fixed on the darkest corners of the room, where the shadows seemed to throb with a malevolent pulse.

Jaime's movements hesitated, her breath hitching audibly in the tense air. "Dee, I—"

"Now!" Dee's command tore from him, a desperate plea laced with urgency. The chilling sound of scraping reached a fever pitch, merging with Mimi's macabre laughter that seemed to come from everywhere at once.

With a frantic urgency, Jaime scrambled at the dresser, the sound of wood scraping against wood piercingly loud as she dismantled their crude barrier. Her breathing was ragged, each breath a sharp stab of sound in the quiet room, her movements frantic and disjointed with fear.

Every second stretched into an eternity as Dee stood guard, every muscle coiled tight, ready to strike or flee. The oppressive darkness of the room pressed in on them, laden with threats unseen but deeply felt, each shadow a cloak for horrors untold.

Dee's muscles were drawn taut, his senses heightened to every whisper of movement as the shadows around them seemed to pulsate with a dark, threatening intent. His fingers tightened around the hammer, the tool's heft reassuring yet inadequate against the terror that Mimi embodied.

Jaime, grappling with the dresser, sent it scraping across the floor in a desperate bid to block the door. The harsh grating noise it made was like a siren call to the horror they faced. Dee's knuckles whitened as he gripped his makeshift weapon, his heart thundering a relentless, pounding rhythm.

Then, cutting through the tension like a blade, Mimi's broken visage appeared from the gloom. The moonlight played cruelly across her cracked porcelain mask, tracing the web of fissures that Jaime's earlier attack had inflicted. It cast her features in a ghastly display, reminiscent of tears carved from shadows.

In her grip shone the dull gleam of a metal rod, sharpened to a deadly point, poised with malevolent intent.

"Move, fucking move!" Dee barked, his voice a ragged edge of urgency directed at Jaime. Behind him, the dresser's scraping crescendoed into a frantic pace.

Mimi's head canted at an eerie angle, her giggle—a chilling, metallic sound—rising in pitch and madness. She advanced, the sway of her tattered dress syncing with her disjointed movements.

With a grunt of effort, Dee swung the hammer in a wide, desperate arc. The air hissed as the tool sliced empty space; Mimi had darted aside with her unnerving agility, her laughter echoing mockingly.

His pulse spiked as she lunged, the sharpened rod aiming straight for his throat. Reflexively, Dee brought the hammer up in defense, the wooden handle meeting metal with a bone-jarring clash that reverberated up his arms.

In the scant heartbeat that followed, Dee's survival instincts surged. He kicked out, catching Mimi off balance. She staggered back, her movements suddenly frantic as she flailed against the unexpected force.

She crashed into a large, cracked mirror on the wall. The impact was catastrophic, splintering the glass with a resounding crash that filled the room with the sound of a thousand icicles breaking. Mimi fell forward into the shattered reflections, the rod slipping from her grasp and skittering across the floor to rest at Dee's feet.

As she tried to right herself, the moonlight cast a macabre ballet of light across the broken glass strewn around her. Each shard mirrored a fragment of her distorted mask, creating a kaleidoscope of twisted smiles that flickered menacingly. Dee stood frozen for a moment, surrounded by the glistening fragments, each piece reflecting not just Mimi's mask but the fractured desperation of their plight.

In the moonlit aftermath of shattered glass, Mimi ascended with a grace that belied her violent intent. Her arms, marred by glistening trails of blood, contrasted starkly against her gown's deeper shade of crimson. Clutched in her hand, a shard of mirror caught the faint light, its jagged edge gleaming with menace.

Dee, muscles coiled with tension, hoisted his hammer once more. His grip, slick with the mingling of sweat and blood, fought for purchase on the worn handle. The once reassuring weight of the hammer now dragged at his arms like an anchor.

As Mimi approached, her head cocked in that unnervingly unnatural angle, her eerie giggle echoed in the cramped space, tunneling into Dee's psyche with maddening persistence.

He swung with desperate might, the hammer carving through the air. But Mimi, with her disturbing agility, simply flowed aside, her movements mocking his effort. The hammer's head met the bedframe instead, sending a jarring reverberation up Dee's arms, threatening to wrench the tool from his grasp.

Pain lanced through Dee as Mimi's makeshift weapon sliced into his bicep, opening a deep, searing wound. Blood welled forth, slick and warm, weakening his grip further.

His subsequent swing was a gambit of sheer desperation, poorly aimed and faltering. Mimi slipped beneath its trajectory with a dancer's grace, her shard of glass plunging into his abdomen with chilling precision.

Dee's legs gave way, his body succumbing to the betrayal of its own strength. As he collapsed, the hammer clattered to the floor, its thud echoing in the hollow silence of the room.

Mimi's figure hovered over him, her movements now bearing a haunting gentleness, as if soothing a restless child. The mask, cracked and leering, framed a vision of darkness within its eye holes—a depth that seemed to stretch back into time itself.

A final flash of the mirrored blade was the last thing Dee saw as it arced towards his throat, a swift, ruthless motion that promised oblivion. Pain erupted in a fierce, bright flood, then ebbed swiftly away as his senses dimmed. The cold floor met his falling body, his lifeblood creating a macabre tableau around him.

In his fading consciousness, Dee's thoughts flickered to Jaime, an image of her face the last wisp of solace as darkness claimed him utterly, the sounds of Mimi's chilling laughter mingling with the ghostly echoes of his final heartbeat.

In the murk of the mansion's labyrinthine corridors, Jess heard the panicked thrum of footsteps before Jaime burst from the shadows, her expression wild and fraught. Jaime's chest heaved as she gasped for air, her voice a shard of desperation piercing the stale air.

"Follow me," Jaime implored, her words taut with urgency.

The plea wrenched at Jess's gut, the raw edge in Jaime's tone echoing the dread swelling in her own chest. Jess cast a fleeting glance at Nichols, noting the white-knuckled grip on his wrench, a silent testament to their shared tension. Micah lingered a step behind, her posture a canvas of defeat.

"What happened?" Jess pressed, her voice tight with foreboding. Jaime, driven by some unseen terror, was already darting back into the darkness.

They trailed Jaime through the mansion's veins, their flashlight beams a chaotic dance across crumbling wallpaper. The acrid scent of blood, metallic and invasive, intensified with each hurried step. Jess's heartbeat was a drumroll against her ribs as they neared a door left ajar.

Jaime thrust the door open with a shove, revealing the chaos within. Jess's gaze snapped first to the mirror's shattered remnants, spread across the floor like ice on winter pavement. Then, heart sinking, she saw Dee.

"No," she breathed out, a whisper lost in the room's oppressive silence.

Dee lay supine, his throat a brutal landscape of violence, his hammer flung just out of reach. His eyes, wide open, mirrored the shock of his final agony.

Jess sank to her knees beside him, her hands suspended above his still form, trembling as if to touch him might confirm this grim reality. "Dee," she murmured, the name a futile invocation in the void he'd left behind.

Nichols prowled the room with ghostly solemnity, his flashlight's beam probing the lingering shadows. "She's gone," he stated, voice devoid of its usual command, replaced by a spectral hollowness. "But she'll be back. She's always fucking back."

Micah approached Jaime, who remained immobile in the doorway, her eyes locked on Dee's corpse.

"What happened?" she asked, her tone a gentle probe.

Jaime's response was distant, her focus tethered to the lifeless form on the floor. "He tried to save me," she murmured, her words trailing into the charged air.

A childlike giggle, chillingly incongruous, reverberated through the mansion, slicing through the dense atmosphere of mourning. The sound, omnipresent and mocking, sent a shiver down Jess's spine, manifesting as goosebumps across her skin.

As the laughter dwindled to a sinister quiet, they were left in a heavy silence, punctuated only by their shallow breaths and the palpable presence of their grief. Surrounded by the echoes of their last companion's attempt at heroism, they faced the harrowing truth: they might be next.

INFERNO OF THE HUNTED

J ess's fingers clung to the crumbling edge of an old table, her knuckles stark white against the weathered wood. Reality seemed to twist and warp around her, a living nightmare from which she couldn't escape. Dee's blood, a vivid reminder of their grim reality, still stained her jeans.

"We can't just keep running and hiding," she declared, her voice a mixture of fear and resolve, a shaky attempt at sounding determined. "We need a solid plan, or none of us are getting out of here alive."

Nichols stood by the window, the weak moonlight straining through the boarded-up gaps, casting shadows across his hardened features like jail bars. He gripped his wrench, his jaw clenched so tightly Jess thought it might crack.

"The plan is simple," he growled, the strain evident in his voice as if fighting back the weight of their dire circumstances. "We find that psychotic bitch and finish this. No more running."

Micah, hugging herself tightly, rocked slightly on her heels. "How, exactly? She knows this place like the back of her hand. We're blind in here," her voice trembled, highlighting the stark fear they all felt.

"We overpower her," Nichols shot back, his proposal ringing hollow in the thick, musty air of the room. "We corner her and take her down as a group—"

"Like Josh did? Or Tadd? Or Dee?" Jaime cut in, her voice escalating to a near shriek, her eyes darting around as if expecting the walls themselves to leap forward. "They were alone, and look what happened! She's hunting us, picking us off one by one, and you want to just charge at her with a wrench?"

Her sarcasm stung with truth, echoing painfully in the dense air. Before Nichols could retort, a chilling, sing-song laugh infiltrated the room, seeping through the thin cracks of the plaster and wood. It twisted around them, a spectral presence that felt as if it emanated from every shadowed corner simultaneously. Jess's hand tightened around her cell phone, its feeble glow a pitiful shield against the enveloping darkness.

"She's here," Jess breathed out, her voice just above a whisper, lost beneath the palpable beat of her own heart, throbbing loud in her ears as fear gripped them all anew.

Jess's pulse thundered in her ears as she surveyed the chaos of the decrepit room, the remnants of shattered lives cluttering every corner. Her fingers wrapped around the cold, rusted metal of a fire poker, its solid heft grounding her amid the disarray.

Beside her, Micah's hands clutched a hefty brass candlestick, her eyes wide with the raw edge of fear. Jaime, with a ragged piece of wood gripped tight, scanned the shadows, every muscle tensed for action.

Nichols stooped, retrieving a half-used can of cleaning spray from under the rubble of a broken chair, his other hand producing a battered silver lighter. His voice was a low growl, laden with intent. "Corner her," he hissed, thumbing the lighter open. "And light her up."

Jess recoiled, her stomach churning. "Burn her alive?" The words tasted bitter, spiked with revulsion.

"You got a better plan?" Nichols shot back, his gaze sharp and merciless under the pale moonlight filtering through the cracked windows. "After everything she's done?"

A deliberate creak from the floorboards outside stilled their hurried preparations. Jess tightened her grip on the poker, her breath shallow, as Micah and Jaime nervously shoved the heavy dresser from the barricaded door.

The door creaked open slowly, ominously. Mimi's silhouette hovered in the frame, her movements eerily fluid, the cracked mask a ghastly beacon in the dim light. Her voice, chillingly childlike, filled the room. "Hide and seek is over... Time to play a new game."

With a grace that belied her malice, Mimi surged forward. Jess ducked just in time, the blade slicing through the air inches from her neck. She retaliated with a desperate swing of the poker, striking Mimi's shoulder and eliciting a scream not of this world.

Jaime lunged, her makeshift weapon swinging; Mimi twisted, dodging with unnatural agility. Her blade danced again, slashing across Jaime's arm, drawing a bright line of pain. Micah attacked with the candlestick, her blow making Mimi stumble b ack.

"Now!" Jess cried out.

Nichols's action was swift—a spray of cleaner jetted forth, ignited by the flick of his lighter into a fiery barrier. Mimi's scream morphed into something monstrous as she recoiled, her mask reflecting the sudden, violent light as she disappeared into the consuming darkness, her laughter lingering, mocking their fleeting victory.

They stood, panting, surrounded by the acrid smell of burnt chemicals and lingering fear, knowing this respite was just that—temporary in their nightmarish ordeal.

In the narrow hallway, Jess clutched the fire poker until her knuckles whitened, her other hand trailing the cool wall. The musty scent of decay filled the air, intensified by the hiss of Nichols's cleaning spray, which left a chemical trail like breadcrumbs in a poisoned forest. Each pulse throbbed against her temples, the drumbeat of their perilous march into Mimi's lair.

Shadows warped by their flashlight beams morphed ordinary debris into monstrous figures, each groan of the old mansion's bones piercing Jess's senses like threats whispered in the dark. The walls seemed to close in, the wallpaper's curled edges reaching towards them with silent, spectral fingers.

"We should go back," Micah's voice was a frayed whisper behind her.

"This is madness," Micah added, her words quivering in the heavy air.

"Keep it together and keep moving," Jaime's voice was a sharp push, physical in its intensity as she nudged Micah roughly forward.

Jess turned, her instincts primed to intervene, but a flicker at the corridor's end snared her attention. A ghostly silhouette coalesced from the gloom—Mimi, appearing as if woven from the darkness itself.

Her attack was a flash of silver, a blade arcing through the dim light to slice across Nichols's arm. Blood spattered the wall, bright against the drab surroundings, its iron tang mingling instantly with the acrid bite of chemicals.

Nichols staggered but regained his footing, his face contorting not just in pain but in fierce determination. He countered with a spray of cleaner aimed directly at Mimi's masked face, the droplets catching the dim light as they settled on the cracked porcelain.

The corridor was split by a grotesque shriek, Mimi stumbling back, her form jerking in a macabre dance. Her laughter, though strangled by agony, still filled the space, retreating with her into the enveloping darkness.

"You'll have to do better than that," she sang back to them, her voice warping around the corners of the hall, a taunt that seemed to seep from the very walls.

As Nichols fumbled, his fingers slick with his own blood, the metallic snap of the lighter echoed hollowly down the shadowed hallway. His movements were desperate, erratic, fueled by pain and fading resolve.

Suddenly, Mimi surged from the darkness, her form a ghastly blur. Her blade gleamed, sweeping towards Nichols with lethal intent. He recoiled, igniting the lighter in a frantic, last-ditch effort. The fine mist of cleaning spray that escaped met the spark, and the hallway was abruptly alight.

Flames erupted with a ferocious roar, engulfing the space between them in a ravenous inferno. Mimi was momentarily enveloped, her shriek piercing the chaos, warped and inhuman. But it was Nichols who bore the brunt of this fiery assault. The flames, hungry and indiscriminate, clung to him, climbing his arm with terrifying speed.

Jess's scream was a ragged tear in the fabric of the moment, filled with horror and disbelief. "No!" Her voice was a raw, tearing sound, almost lost beneath the crackle and hiss of the fire.

Nichols collapsed, his body an agonizing pyre. The can of spray tumbled from his grasp, clanging uselessly to the ground. His screams—terrifying in their intensity—filled the corridor, a sound so primal and pained that it clawed at Jess's very soul.

Through the blaze, Jess's eyes met the charred remnants of Mimi's mask. The twisted grin, now a grotesque parody amidst the flames, seemed to leer at them, triumphant and monstrous, before she retreated back into the suffocating darkness of the mansion.

Jaime recoiled, horror struck, her hands dropping the makeshift club. It thudded dully on the floor, forgotten. In her eyes, the reflection of the fire danced wildly, painting her features with the light of utter terror.

On the floor, Nichols's body twitched horrifically, his cries dwindling to choked sobs as the fire consumed him. The thick, bitter stench of burning flesh and synthetic material rapidly filled the air, a tangible reminder of the nightmare unfolding around them. The fire crackled and spat, a monstrous entity in its own right, devouring all it touched with insatiable greed.

Smoke choked the air, burning Jess's lungs as she coughed and gasped for breath. Nichols's tortured screams had dwindled to nothing more than gurgling whispers, barely audible over the crackling fire. Through the haze, Mimi's figure emerged, her movements eerily smooth against the backdrop of chaos. The mask on her face, blackened and warped from the heat, caught the light of the flames, reflecting them as if part of some grotesque carnival.

"Such pretty colors," Mimi cooed, her voice unnervingly calm as she observed the fiery destruction. "Red and orange and blue, just like Mother's garden..." Her words, twisted with delight, floated eerily through the turmoil.

Jess felt a surge of fury ignite within her, momentarily overcoming her dread. "You fucking monster!" she screamed, launching the fire poker with all the force her smoke-weary muscles could muster. The metal implement sailed through the air, missing Mimi as she deftly slipped back into the shadows, her disturbing giggle trailing after her.

"Move!" Jess barked, her voice hoarse as she seized Jaime's arm, pulling her forward with desperate urgency. "We need to go, now!"

Micah, pale and trembling, clutched at Jaime's other side. "We can't leave him—" she began, her voice breaking.

"He's gone!" Jess interrupted with conviction, her tone brooking no argument as she tugged them both toward the safety of the opposite hallway. "There's nothing we can do for him now."

They raced away from the scene, the heavy smoke billowing behind them like a vengeful specter, carrying the vile scent of charred flesh. Nichols's body was left behind, consumed by flames—a grim reminder of Mimi's lethal caprice.

In the labyrinthine darkness of the mansion's hallways, Jess stumbled forward, her phone's feeble light barely cutting through the oppressive gloom. Each breath scorched her lungs, a brutal reminder of Nichols's fiery demise, his screams still echoing in her ears. Behind her, the flickering orange from his inferno cast monstrous shadows that danced macabrely along the peeling, ancient wallpaper.

"Left," she choked out, yanking Jaime and Micah around yet another corner into the maze-like heart of the old house.

Jaime's flashlight swung erratically, brushing over family portraits defaced with dark, hollow eyes that seemed to follow them. Micah's light flickered perilously, nearly drowning them in darkness before she thumped it against her hand, coaxing a steady glow that mingled with the distant firelight, casting eerie shadows.

A sinister giggle, too sweet and too close, echoed down the corridors, curling around them like a cold whisper. Mimi was playing with them, drawing them deeper into her deadly game.

"In here," Jess directed, spotting a sturdy wooden door. She yanked it open, revealing a room shrouded in shadows that might have once offered refuge as a bedroom. They stumbled in, panting from fear and exertion.

Jess slammed the door with a force that resounded through the room, reverberating against every corner. Her hands trembled as she grabbed an ancient dresser. "Help me," she demanded, her voice raw with desperation.

Together, they heaved the heavy furniture against the door, the legs scraping grotesquely over the rotting wood, securing their temporary barricade. They collapsed against it, breathless, their sweat mingling with tears.

Jaime slid down against the wall, her resolve crumbling. "We're going to die here," she murmured, the fight draining out of her as she covered her face with her hands, her voice broken. "Just like Dee. Just like all of them."

Micah stood numbly, her gaze fixed on the wall, her body barely seeming to breathe, lit by the eerie, stuttering pulse of her flashlight. Her silhouette flickered, ghost-like, casting a specter of dread that painted her as another lost soul of the mansion.

Exhausted and engulfed by despair, Jess leaned heavily against the dresser, the slight glow from her phone casting long, ominous shadows across the room. The low battery warning flashed, a cruel reminder of their dwindling lifeline. Her voice, barely a whisper, carried the weight of their grim reality.

"Jaime might be right."

Deception in the Darkness

J ess's pulse hammered, a frantic tattoo against her ribcage as the sharp tang of chemicals bit into her nostrils. Her phone's faint glow illuminated the slick of liquid seeping beneath the door, spreading a sinister stain across the decaying wood.

"Gas," she gasped, the word barely a whisper, as she seized Micah's arm, her fingers digging in desperately. "We need to move. Now!"

With a grunt of effort, Jaime wrenched the dresser from the door, her movements heavy with urgency. Jess's eyes stung as the chemical fumes thickened, blurring her vision. She wrenched the door open, and the hallway stretched before them, an endless maw ready to consume them.

In the thickening darkness behind, the scratch of a match flared, casting a brief, eerie light on

Mimi's grotesquely cracked mask. Jess shoved Micah ahead, propelling her through the doorway with force born of sheer terror. The match sputtered out, extinguished with a faint, ominous hiss.

"Run!" Jess's scream ripped from her throat, raw and hoarse. Her phone's light jerked madly as she sprinted down the corridor, the shadows morphing into menacing figures clawing at the edges of the beam. The floorboards groaned under her frantic steps, threatening to splinter and collapse beneath her.

Behind, Micah faltered, her own light slashing wildly at the walls as she struggled to breathe. "I can't—I can't keep going—"

"Move your ass!" Jaime's command was a fierce growl as she clutched Micah's arm, dragging her forward with relentless determination. Her flashlight swung wildly, probing the suffocating darkness for signs of their tormentor. "She's right behind us!"

At the periphery of Jess's faltering light, a shadow twitched—an elusive whisper of movement. Her stomach clenched with dread. Then, chillingly clear, a childlike voice echoed through the hall.

"Ring around the rosie," Mimi's sing-song taunt reverberated off the damp walls, a nursery rhyme turned sinister. "Pockets full of posies..."

Jess halted, her breath catching in her throat, the cold grip of fear paralyzing her. The light from her phone revealed only the desolation of the decaying corridor, no sign of Mimi, yet her presence was palpable, a malevolent force enveloping them.

Mimi's laughter, grotesquely distorted, erupted from the darkness, morphing from playful to predatory in the blink of an eye. The sound raised the fine hairs on Jess's neck, a primal warning of imminent danger.

"Please," Micah sobbed next to her, her voice breaking with raw terror. "Please, I don't want to die here."

The dire situation, their isolation, and the encroaching danger melded into a palpable terror that clung to Jess like a second skin, driving them onward, deeper into the nightmarish depths of the mansion.

Jess's throat tightened as Micah's sobs echoed down the hallway, the sound a sharp reminder of their dire predicament. The burden of their desperate situation weighed heavily on Jess, each breath an effort under the crushing despair. She had to make a decision—now.

"Run! Both of you, run!" Jess's voice shattered the oppressive silence as she pushed Micah ahead. The beam from her phone sliced through the darkness, a fleeting guide along the decaying corridor.

Micah's sneakers squealed against the rotting floorboards as she lunged forward. Hope flickered briefly—then Jaime's foot lashed out, tripping Micah with cruel precision.

Micah hit the floor hard, the impact sending a sickening thud echoing off the walls. The brass candlestick she clutched flew from her grasp, skittering into the dark recesses of the hallway. Her flashlight tumbled away, its light flailing wildly across the peeling wallpaper before it flickered and died.

"Micah!" Jess surged forward, but Jaime's grip clamped around her wrist like a vise.

"Keep running," Jaime ordered, her fingers digging painfully into Jess's skin. "Don't stop."

On the floor, Micah struggled to her knees, blood dribbling from a split lip. Her tears made clean streaks through the dirt on her face as she reached out imploringly. "Please," she whimpered. "Please don't leave me."

In the dim light from Jess's phone, a shadow detached itself from the darker recesses of the hallway. Mimi stepped forward, her cracked porcelain mask catching the frail light. She held a rusted cast-iron skillet with a childlike fascination, her head cocked as if curious about its weight.

Jess's mouth opened in a silent scream of warning, but it was too late. Mimi swung the skillet in a brutal arc, the metal connecting with a sickening crack against Micah's temple.

Blood arced through the air, splattering the floor with a gruesome spray. Mimi struck again, relentless, each blow delivered with the precision of a machine, the sick thuds chillingly methodical.

Frozen in horror, Jess could only watch as the deadly ballet unfolded before her. Her hands shook so violently that her phone almost slipped through her fingers, the light trembling, making the horrific scene strobe in nightmarish flashes.

Jaime's pull on Jess's arm snapped her back to reality. "She was dead weight anyway," Jaime's voice was cold, emotionless. "Now let's go."

The raw dismissal of Micah's life hit Jess like a physical blow, leaving her numbed as she allowed herself to be pulled away, the haunting echo of Mimi's giggle chasing them into the dark.

Jess stumbled after Jaime, each step a battle against the urge to collapse. The metallic stench of Micah's blood lingered, a cruel reminder, mixed with the acrid bite of chemical residues. Her phone's light careened off the walls, sending monstrous shadows twisting through the corridor.

"We killed her," Jess murmured, her voice breaking under the weight of realization. "We left her to die."

"Shut the fuck up and keep moving." Jaime's command sliced through the thick darkness, her tone sharp and unforgiving. Her footsteps clattered ahead, relentless and quick.

"She begged us—" Jess choked on the memory, the gruesome soundtrack of Micah's end replaying in her mind, each blow a wet thud that sank deeper into her consciousness.

"She was dead weight." Jaime's retort came harshly as she glanced back, her figure a fleeting shadow against the dim glow of Jess's phone. "Better her than us."

They burst into another room, Jaime slamming the door with a force that shook its decaying frame.

Overcome, Jess slumped to the ground, the cold floor a hard reality beneath her. Her phone skittered away, its light flickering and then steadying, casting an eerie glow. She buried her face in her hands, her body wracked with silent sobs. The room closed in around them, the silence a heavy shroud, broken only by their labored breathing and the occasional eerie creak of the old mansion settling into the night.

Jess's gaze fixed on Jaime through the haunting glow of her phone, a torrent of rage swelling in her chest with each heartbeat. The pungent metallic scent of Micah's blood lingered, an unwelcome reminder in the stale air of their grim sanctuary. Jess's fingers trembled, her mind replaying the harrowing scene—Jaime's calculated move, Micah's abrupt fall, the horrifying sound of metal colliding with flesh.

"You tripped her," Jess spat out, her voice low and laced with venom, the words burning her throat as they escaped.

Jaime leaned nonchalantly against the wall, the shadows partially obscuring her expression, but the chill in her eyes was unmistakable. "She was weak. We're still breathing because I did what was necessary," she retorted, her voice dripping with cold pragmatism.

That cavalier disregard for Micah's life set off a visceral reaction in Jess. She surged from her crouched position, her hands balling into fists so tightly that her nails dug painfully into her palms. "You don't have the right to decide who lives and dies!" she thundered, stepping closer to Jaime.

Jaime advanced with a menacing calm, her eyes a pair of hostile embers in the dim light. She pushed Jess forcefully, sending her staggering back against the heavy dresser. The sharp pain from the impact jolted through Jess's body.

Regaining her balance, Jess lunged forward, propelled by raw anger. Her voice escalated, filled with scorn and outrage. "You're a monster!" she accused, her every word saturated with disdain.

Jaime's forceful shove sent Jess staggering back, her spine slamming against the dresser with a sharp crack that reverberated through her bones. Pain flared across her back, but it was the surge of fury that dominated, igniting her resolve. With a fierce grunt, she surged forward, seizing Jaime by the shoulders and thrusting her against the wall with a force that dislodged a cloud of dust from the decaying wallpaper.

"You murdered her!" Jess's voice was a raw, animalistic growl, her fingers pressing painfully into Jaime's shoulders. "She trusted us!"

In retaliation, Jaime's knee thrust upward into Jess's stomach, driving the breath from her in a violent whoosh. Stars exploded in Jess's vision as she doubled over, vulnerable. Jaime's fist clipped her cheekbone, sending Jess staggering sideways.

"Trust gets you killed here!" Jaime snarled, spitting a streak of blood onto the gritty floor. Her eyes were wild, illuminated by fury and fear in the scant light. "You want to end up like Micah? Like Dee?"

Dee's name reignited a fierce blaze within Jess. With a roar, she charged, tackling Jaime to the ground. The impact was harsh, and Jess's elbow smashed into Jaime's nose with a crunch, spattering her own hand with blood.

Jaime retaliated fiercely, her nails carving painful lines across Jess's face. They writhed on the floor, their bodies a whirl of violence as they struck each other, each blow echoing with a sinister tone in the cramped space. The taste of iron flooded Jess's mouth as blood welled from her injuries.

Jess managed to break free from the brutal dance, her hands scrambling across the floor, searching, until her fingers wrapped around the cold metal of the flashlight. As she seized it, Jaime lunged, grabbing at Jess's ankle. Jess kicked fiercely, her heel connecting solidly with Jaime's face, breaking her hold.

With a swift motion, Jess was at the door, wrenching it open. Her face was slick with blood, her lip split and swelling as she turned, the flashlight's beam slicing through the dense air.

"Go to hell," Jess snarled, her voice a hoarse whisper of rage and defiance. "I hope Mimi finds you first."

She didn't wait for a response, stepping into the hallway, her form enveloped by the oppressive shadows. The door thudded shut behind her, her footsteps a rapid, fading echo as she disappeared into the labyrinthine darkness of the mansion, each step taking her further into the unknown.

Jaime's heart thundered painfully in her chest as she slammed her fist against the crumbling wall, her voice cracking the stagnant air, "Fuck you, Jess!" The words, heavy with betrayal and hurt, reverberated off the stripped wallpaper and shattered remnants of furniture that cluttered the room. Each breath she drew felt sharper, more desperate as the last echoes of their confrontation faded into a suffocating silence.

"Shit." The expletive slipped from her lips as she fumbled through her pocket, her hands shaking uncontrollably as she managed to activate the flashlight on her phone. Its feeble glow sliced through the oppressive darkness, casting elongated, sinister shadows that danced across the decaying floorboards.

A soft creak from outside the door snagged her already frayed nerves. Was it merely the house settling, or was it something more sinister? Her pulse quickened, each beat a loud drum in her ears. Another creak, undeniably closer this time, confirmed her fears.

Dry-mouthed with trepidation, Jaime approached the door. Her fingers wrapped tightly around the doorknob, the metal cool and slick with her sweat. She turned it slowly, painstakingly, the slight squeal of the hinges sounding monstrously loud in the heavy silence.

The door creaked open, revealing the shadow-drenched hallway. Her phone's beam sliced through the darkness, illuminating swirling dust motes that seemed to hover in the air like spectral entities. At first glance, the corridor appeared empty—a void of decay and desolation.

Then, the beam settled on a figure lurking motionless in the corner. Mimi. Her porcelain mask, grotesquely beautiful, reflected the light with a sinister sheen, marred by the dark stains of Micah's blood. In her hands, she clutched a pair of rusted hedge shears, their blades long and menacing, scraping against the wooden floor as she shifted her stance. Her head was cocked in an unnatural angle, reminiscent of a doll broken and discarded.

The scraping of metal intensified as Mimi began to advance towards Jaime, each step deliberate, the sound mingling eerily with her chilling, childlike giggles. Jaime's breath hitched, her throat constricting with fear as the masked figure drew nearer, the hedge shears dragging deep, angry gouges into the ancient wood, heralding her approach.

CUTTING TIES

As Jaime felt the weight of her impending doom, the cold hallway seemed to close in around her, the scraping of Mimi's hedge shears against the decaying wood of the floor sending a visceral shudder through her body. Her phone's light flickered, the battery warning flashing as a harbinger of her fading hope.

"Jess!" Her voice shattered the ominous silence, a desperate plea for redemption. "Jess, please! I'm sorry!" The echo of her own words taunted her, the halls returning only the sinister drag of metal on wood as Mimi inched closer.

The moonlight struggled through the dirt-streaked windows, catching the grotesque details of the porcelain mask—its surface webbed with cracks and the dark, dried remnants of Micah's blood painting a morbid mask of war. Mimi's head canted to a disturbing angle, suggesting a neck snapped and wrongly reset.

Jaime backed into the unyielding wall, her facade cracking as she forced a nervous smile. "Hey, list en... we can work something out, right?" Her voice wavered, betraying her fear. "I mean, I get it. This is your home. We shouldn't have come here."

The metallic dance of the shears ceased abruptly. Mimi stood still, her form a spectral silhouette framed by shadows, the shears hanging ominously by her side.

"I could... I could help you," Jaime stammered, her plea laced with desperation. "Keep others away. Make sure no one else bothers you." She swallowed the lump in her throat, the taste of fear sharp on her tongue. "Just let me go. Please."

A perverse tilt of the head was Mimi's only response, her neck emitting a sickening crack that echoed softly in the stale air. A childlike giggle, unnerving in its innocence, filled the room as Mimi slowly lifted the shears, the blades catching the last desperate flickers of light from Jaime's phone.

"Please," Jaime whispered, the finality of her situation sinking in, her voice a mere breath in the vast darkness. "I don't want to die."

Jaime's spine pressed hard against the wall, each heartbeat a thunderous echo in her chest. In the dwindling light of her phone, Mimi's blood-streaked dress appeared even more sinister. Desperation clawed at Jaime's voice as she pitched her last, frantic gambit. "Wait," she gasped, her hand trembling as she raised it. "I know where Jess went. I can lead you to her." The lie burned her tongue, bile rising in her throat. "She's the real threat, isn't she? The fighter?"

Sweat streamed down Jaime's back, her breath ragged as she scrambled to spin her deceit further. "Let me bring her to you. She trusts me—or she did, until..." Her words faltered as the gruesome image of Micah's end haunted her thoughts.

The mask on Mimi's face seemed to absorb the scant light, her head tilting curiously, the shears pausing their ominous dance against the floor. Jaime's pulse quickened as she wove her narrative, each word laced with a toxic blend of fear and manipulation. "Jess thinks she's better than us, always judging, always in control. Wouldn't you relish the chance to break her? To see the betrayal on her face when she realizes it's me who led her to you?"

For a moment, Mimi's mask remained impassive, the porcelain eerily still in the half-light. Then, subtly, it tilted, the skeletal creak of her neck breaking the heavy silence. "Help?" The word came out distorted, a twisted echo of Jaime's proposal, laden with dark amusement.

Jaime's heart skipped as Mimi leaned closer, the grotesque smile of the mask inches from her face, the stench of iron and decay overwhelming. "Help... me?" The giggle that followed morphed into a horrifying growl, the sound skittering down Jaime's spine like cold fingers.

A wave of dread submerged Jaime, her stomach plummeting as she realized her gamble had failed. There was no bargaining with this nightmare. Mimi's grip on the hedge shears tightened, the old metal creaking as if in anticipation. The reality that her pleas had fallen on deaf ears—or perhaps no ears at all—settled heavy around her, a shroud that tightened with every shallow breath.

Jaime's heart seized as the hedge shears whistled past her, just grazing the skin of her neck. She staggered back, her feet catching on the decayed carpet. The blades snagged her sleeve, ripping through the fabric with a harsh tear.

"Fuck!" She gasped out the curse, panic spurring her limbs into frantic motion. Her phone slipped from her grasp, skittering across the floor and plunging her world into darkness as it flickered out.

The suffocating blackness enveloped her. Jaime's boots pounded the warped floorboards as she sprinted down the hallway, each echoing step driving her deeper into terror. Behind her, the relentless scrape of metal on wood pursued her, deliberate and chillingly calm.

"Help!" she screamed, her voice shredding in her throat, raw with terror. "Jess, please!"

Her plea echoed mockingly in the empty corridor. Peripheral shadows twisted into monstrous shapes, and the walls throbbed with the cadence of her labored breathing.

She made a sharp left at a junction, her balance faltering on the uneven surface. Darkness stretched interminably before her, sporadically pierced by moonlight filtering through sealed windows. Her lungs scorched with exertion, each breath dragging painfully over her dry throat.

The scraping sound tracked her relentlessly, a leisurely symphony of impending doom. Mimi's giggle, light and horrifying, wove through the darkness, surrounding Jaime, disorienting and omnipresent.

Stumbling over a protruding floorboard, Jaime crashed to the ground. Agony lanced through her palms as they struck the gritty floor. She pushed herself up, ignoring the sting of scraped skin and the warm blood that began to ooze.

She rounded another corner, her frantic escape leading her down yet another foreboding corridor. Moonlight revealed a familiar pattern of peeling wallpaper and broken doorways. A gut-wrenching realization dawned—she was back where she had started.

"No, no, no!" Despair gripped her as she pounded the walls with bloodied fists, wallpaper flaking under her blows. "This can't be happening!"

The metallic scraping crescendoed, drawing ever nearer. Tears blurred her vision, mixing with the sweat and grime on her face as the stark reality settled in. Jaime had run full circle, trapped in an endless nightmare orchestrated by Mimi, who seemed to close in with each second, her childlike laughter echoing as a death knell in the shadowy mansion.

Jaime spun on her heel, her heart slamming into her ribs as she confronted the horrifying tableau at the hallway's end. Mimi stood eerily still, the rusted hedge shears splayed open in her grip like the wings of some predatory bird, moonlight glinting menacingly off the jagged edges. The porcelain mask, tilted at a grotesque angle, reflected the sparse light filtering through the boarded-up windows.

"Pretty little bird," Mimi cooed through the darkness, her voice a twisted lullaby. "Trapped in my cage."

Adrenaline surged through Jaime's veins, propelling her into a desperate sprint in the opposite direction. Her boots thudded against the decaying wood, each step echoing like a drumbeat in her ears. Pain lanced through her legs, weary from the relentless flight, but fear spurred her onward. The mansion's shadows morphed under the meager moonlight, stretching into monstrous shapes along the crumbling walls.

Her breathing was labored, each inhalation a fiery agony, as the endless corridors of the mansion loomed before her, each turn and twist a mocking reminder of her entrapment. Behind her, the sinister sound of shears dragging along the floor marked Mimi's unhurried pursuit, a relentless reminder of the danger at her heels.

"Fuck, fuck, fuck!" Jaime's cries echoed down the empty halls, her voice fracturing in terror. The walls threw her own panic back at her, distorting and amplifying it until it seemed to come from everywhere, enveloping her in a cacophony of fear.

A misplaced step, her foot catching on a warped floorboard, sent Jaime tumbling to the ground. The shock of the hard landing reverberated through her body, pain flaring in her knees as they struck the wood. The air whooshed out of her lungs, leaving her wheezing in the oppressive darkness, her body sprawled helplessly on the cold floor of the mansion.

Jaime's heart battered her ribcage, each beat syncopated with the haunting hum that floated down the darkened corridor. The melody, eerie and out of place, mingled with the sinister scrape of metal dragging across the decaying wood, setting Jaime's nerves on edge.

As she retreated, her bloodied palms left a visceral trail on the rotted boards, each movement etching pain into her raw skin. Mimi's mask, splattered with dried crimson, caught the weak rays of moonlight seeping through the boarded-up windows, casting grotesque shadows across her face.

"Stay back!" Jaime's plea tore through the silence, her voice a shattered whisper against the relentless advance of the shears, their rusted blades catching glimmers of light.

Cornered, with her back against the cold, unyielding wall, Jaime slid to the floor, her legs unable to support her any longer. Mimi's approach was methodical, her blood-stained gown rustling against her legs with each step. The humming intensified, warping into a chilling lullaby that seemed to seep into the very air.

"No, no, no!" Jaime sobbed, the reality of her impending doom crashing down on her. Tears carved clean lines down her dirt-streaked face as she cowered, the wall cold and unforgiving against her spine. "I don't want to die! Please!"

Mimi paused, her head cocking to one side in a grotesquely curious tilt as she crouched to meet

Jaime's gaze. The mask was inches away, its porcelain surface a macabre tableau of fractured innocence. The smell of iron—blood, both old and fresh—was overpowering.

"Pretty bird," Mimi cooed, her voice a disturbing caress in the claustrophobic space. "Time to clip your wings." The shears opened with a slow, deliberate motion, the sound of metal against metal echoing with a foreboding tone as they prepared to strike.

Jaime's arms flailed upward as the shears howled their metallic scream, the sound slicing through the terror-choked atmosphere. The blades, chill and merciless, sank deep into her flesh, igniting trails of excruciating pain that splintered through her body. Blood burst forth in a vivid spray, staining her skin with warm, sticky crimson.

"No, please!" Her plea was a choked gurgle, her muscles writhing in futile defense against the brutal descent of steel.

The mask hovered nearer, moonlight catching its fractured surface, casting eerie shards of light across the space. Mimi's head gave a grotesque tilt, the sound of her bones a macabre symphony. The shears, now gaping menacingly wider, paused as if savoring the fear permeating the air.

A brutal agony tore through Jaime's neck as the shears clamped shut. Her attempt to scream was stifled into a horrifying gurgle as the blades ground against bone, the pressure monstrous in its intensity. Her world blurred, shadows creeping in to claim her sight, her senses drowning in a tide of pain.

The final vision that burned into Jaime's fading consciousness was the ghastly smile of the porcelain mask—a silent observer to her demise. The shears completed their grisly task with a nauseating crunch, severing head from body.

Jaime's head tumbled, tracing a grisly path down the corridor, her lifeblood spattering the walls in grotesque patterns of red. A gruesome fountain of blood spewed from the stump of her neck, painting a macabre mural in the dimly lit hallway.

Above Jaime's mutilated body, Mimi paused, her head cocked in a perverse approximation of curiosity, observing the chaos she had wrought as if it were a grotesque piece of art. The shears dripped with relentless rhythm, contributing to the dark pool spreading on the floor. Then, with the silence of a wraith, she receded into the dense shadows, abandoning Jaime's staring eyes to the cold gaze of the overhead chandelier, their light reflecting a dismal tableau of her last desperate fight for life.

Dead Ends and Despair

In the mansion's suffocating gloom, Jess's limp drew sharp pain through her bruised ribs with each laborious step. The contusions from her violent encounter with Jaime pulsed under her shirt, a relentless reminder of the swift collapse of trust amidst the horror. Her flashlight sliced a narrow path through the darkness, the beam snagging on peeling wallpaper and sinister stains she dared not dwell upon.

With each creak of the ancient floorboards under her weight, Jess halted, her breath caught in her throat. The noise echoed, reverberating through the stark silence around her. Her flashlight flickered, dimming briefly into near-darkness before steadying, casting grotesque shadows that seemed to claw at the air around her.

"Keep it together," she rasped to herself, her voice a harsh whisper that sounded too loud in the enclosing stillness. The encouragement rang empty in the musty corridor.

She continued her tentative advance, eyes scouring the walls for any crack, any small offering of escape. The windows were relentlessly barred; the doors she tested were steadfastly locked or led only to further despair. Each attempt to open another way out sent a lance of pain through her side, the protest of her battered body.

The mansion itself seemed to inhale deeply, walls subtly shifting as if sighing with age—or perhaps that was just her frazzled nerves painting terror where there was none. Faces of the fallen haunted her—a macabre roll call of those she'd lost: Josh, Dee, Nichols, Micah, Tadd. And Jaime, despite the betrayal.

Pressing her ear against the cool, rough plaster, Jess sought to anchor herself by the sounds within these confounding halls. Her own heartbeat thudded oppressively loud in her ears, almost drowning out the world. Then, a chilling sound cut through: footsteps overhead, deliberate and slow, accompanied by the sinister song of metal dragging across wood—the echo of doom she knew all too well.

Rooted to the spot, Jess barely allowed herself to breathe, much less move. The footsteps traced a path directly above her, each thud a hammer blow to her sanity. She was caught in a frozen span of time, each second stretching interminably as she waited for the menace to pass.

Trapped. Jess's heart sank as the stark reality of the dead end assaulted her. Her flashlight, her last lifeline, flickered in protest before succumbing to the darkness that eagerly filled every inch of space around her. "Fuck," she whispered into the suffocating black, the word a soft curse that fluttered away into nothing.

Frantic, she rattled the flashlight, smacking it against her open palm in vain. Darkness clung to her likc a second skin, oppressive and complete. Her fingers traced the cold, rough wall behind her as she attempted to navigate back the way she had come, but splinters dug viciously into her skin, drawing a sharp hiss of pain from her lips. Each step sent a throb of agony through her bruised ribs, the echo of her brutal altercation with Jaime.

Suddenly, a sliver of light beckoned from a crack in the wall to her left. Jess halted, her breath trapped in her throat. Peering through the narrow aperture, she met the fragmented gaze of Mimi's porcelain mask. The cracks in the surface warped the dim light, turning the mask into a grotesque mosaic of shadows and pale luminescence.

A scream clawed at her throat, desperate to escape. Jess clamped a hand over her mouth, stifling the sound as she staggered back into the deeper shadows. Her back met the cold, unforgiving wall as she edged away from the terrifying specter.

The mask shifted slightly, its angle changing as if Mimi's head had cocked to the side, a silent, eerie gesture of curiosity. Jess's heart pounded violently against her ribcage, each beat resonating with the cold dread that Mimi's gaze seemed to penetrate the darkness, seeking her out.

Desperate, Jess pressed herself into the darkest corner she could find, her breaths shallow and silent. The mask lingered at the crack, a sentinel of doom that seemed to watch, wait, and mock her dwindling hopes of escape. Jess prayed for the shadows to envelop her completely, to hide her from the monstrous fate that stalked her so relentlessly.

Jess's fingers trembled against the cold, metallic curve of a doorknob hidden in the darkness. Her heart leaped as she fumbled with her phone, the screen's meager glow casting eerie shadows against the peeling wallpaper of the corridor. The battery indicator blinked a warning red—only 2% remaining.

"Please," she murmured, her voice a breathless whisper as she directed the frail light toward the handle. With a reluctant creak, the brass knob turned, and she stumbled into the doorway. The grand staircase loomed before her, its once-majestic banister now warped and decaying. Strips of moonlight sneaked through the barred windows above, casting shadows like prison bars across the s teps.

Gripping the banister, Jess winced; each breath was a sharp stab of pain in her ribs. The wood under her palm was slick—she dared not think with what. Dust motes caught in the beam of her phone, swirling like spectral dancers in the stale air of the vast hallway.

As she ascended, the stairs groaned under her weight, her shaky legs barely supporting her. Each of her ragged breaths echoed in the stillness, too loud, too conspicuous. Her phone's light flickered ominously, threatening to leave her blind in this vast, decaying tomb.

She had only made it a quarter of the way up when a shadow stirred at the foot of the staircase. Her blood froze.

There stood Mimi, the porcelain mask catching the faint light, reflecting it back as a sickly gleam. Her movements were stiff, unnaturally precise, as she placed one foot on the first step. The hedge shears hung from her hand, the blades dark with wet, fresh blood—Jaime's, perhaps? The very thought twisted Jess's stomach with dread.

The mask was grotesquely tilted, the crack in the porcelain spreading into what seemed like a sinister grin. From below, Mimi's voice drifted up, a childlike whisper that was chilling in its innocence.

Jess's grip tightened on a loose baluster, splinters biting into her skin as she ripped it free. The rotting wood surrendered with a sharp snap, echoing through the stairwell with a sinister tone. Pain lanced through her ribs, a stark reminder of every bruise, every blow she had endured.

Below her, Mimi ascended the staircase, the broken mask eerily catching the moonlight seeping through the barred windows. The hedge shears in her grip glistened with fresh blood, a grotesque reminder of her brutality. With a surge of adrenaline,

Jess swung the wooden baluster with all the force her battered body could muster.

The strike was a solid thud, wood colliding with porcelain. The shock of the impact jolted through Jess's arms as the baluster fractured, pieces splintering apart. Mimi reeled back, her head tilting at an impossible angle, yet she remained on her feet. The mask's cracked grin seemed to stretch further, a network of new fissures webbing across the surface, mocking Jess with its resilience.

"Fuck this." The words were a venomous whisper as Jess flung the remnants of the baluster straight at Mimi's twisted smile. Spinning around, she bounded up the stairs, taking them two at a time. Each breath was a fiery agony in her chest, her ribs screaming in protest with every leap.

The relentless rhythm of Mimi's pursuit echoed behind her—a methodical click and scrape of metal against wood. The sound was a chilling metronome, each note a reminder of the hunter's unyielding advance. There was no haste in Mimi's movements, only the steady, terrifying certainty of a predator confident in its hunt.

"Where are you going?" Mimi's voice, sing-song and horrifyingly playful, floated up the stairwell. "Don't you want to play with me?" The words twisted in the gloom, intertwining with the shadows that seemed to clutch at Jess with spectral fingers.

Jess's heart pounded against her ribs, her breaths sharp and ragged as she dared not look back, her every sense screaming that to do so would be to face the abyss itself.

Jess reached the landing, her breaths harsh and ragged, the pain in her ribs pulsing with each heaving gasp. Moonlight sneaked through the barred windows, throwing long, sinister shadows across a landscape of decay: a shattered desk, overturned filing cabinets, chairs with their upholstery gutted like fish. A room with no exits, a trap laid bare.

Her curse was a whisper of despair, "Fuck, fuck, fuck," as she spun to face the staircase. Below, Mimi's footsteps marked a steady, metallic rhythm of impending doom—the scrape of the hedge shears against the steps sounded like the tick of a clock counting down her life.

Her eyes snapped to a heavy wooden chair by a dust-covered window. Pain shot through her side as she heaved the chair, dragging its legs with a grating sound across the decayed floor to the head of the stairs.

Mimi emerged into view, the dim light playing off her mask, highlighting the spiderweb of cracks from their last encounter. Her smile, a frozen grimace of distorted joy, seemed to widen. She ascended, each step deliberate, the shears dripping dark, viscous blood onto the wood.

"Stay back!" Jess's voice was hoarse, strained with terror as she pushed the chair. It toppled, gaining deadly momentum as it crashed down the stairs.

The collision was catastrophic. Mimi was struck off-balance, her body contorting grotesquely as she fell backward. The shears flew from her grip, clanging against the walls. Her descent was a series of brutal thuds, each one a chilling punctuation to Jess's pounding heart.

Mimi landed with a final, sickening crunch at the base of the staircase, crumpled and unnaturally still. Blood began seeping out, darkening the wood beneath her shattered mask.

Jess's knees buckled, and she crumpled onto the landing, her body shaking from exertion and shock. Breathing was agony; every inhale was a knife in her chest. Sweat mingled with tears as she wiped her face, trying to regain some semblance of control.

Time lost meaning as she stared down at the wreckage of her tormentor, at the life she might have just ended. Gathering her strength, Jess descended the stairs, her steps wary as she navigated around the chaotic aftermath of her desperate act.

The hedge shears lay discarded, a reminder of the violence, coated with Jaime's blood. Reaching the bottom, Jess hesitated, her gaze locked on Mimi's still form. The growing pool of blood reached the hem of her tattered dress, seeping into the fabric.

A glint of metal caught Jess's eye—an almost hidden chain around Mimi's neck. She whispered, hopeful, "Please be what I think it is." Her hands shook as she reached for it, pulling at the chain until a rusted key came free with a snap that seemed to fill the silence of the house.

"Front door key." The words were a prayer. She clutched the key, its cold metal a solid promise in her palm, as she turned to face the door that now represented her final escape.

Jess's progression towards the front door was a march of pain, each step reigniting the fire in her battered ribs. The mansion's darkness seemed almost sentient, disturbed only by sporadic moonbeams slicing through barred windows. Her legs shook under the strain of endless hours of evasion and conflict, her muscles howling with fatigue.

A ghastly sight halted her—a glimpse of pale flesh. There lay Jaime's severed head, settled in a darkening pool of blood, her eyes that once sparkled with defiance now dull and vacant. Her dark hair, clotted with blood, formed a grim halo around her stark face. Nausea surged within Jess, bile climbing her throat; she wrenched her gaze away, heart pounding against the hollow of despair.

The front door stood before her, a testament to years of abandonment, marred and forsaken. Jess's hands trembled as she raised the rusted key to the lock. It scraped against metal, stubbornly resisting entry.

"Come on," she urged under her breath, her fingers awkwardly maneuvering the key. It grated against the lock, unwilling to turn. She twisted it desperately, hope dwindling with each failed attempt.

"No." The word was a whisper of defeat. "No, no, no," she cried, her voice breaking as she forced the key with trembling ferocity. The lock groaned under the pressure but remained locked tight.

A chilling realization washed over her, cold and merciless—the key was not for the front door. All the horrors, all the deaths, and escape was still a mocking mirage. Her legs gave way, and she collapsed against the door, sliding down its unforgiving surface to the cold floor.

Her phone slipped from her grasp, its light flickering out as the screen blanked—a finality that mirrored the snuffing of hope. Darkness enveloped her completely as she buried her head in her arms, her body wracked with silent, convulsive sobs. The silence of the mansion enveloped her, punctured only by her uneven breaths and a distant laughter—Mimi's haunting echoes, whether real or conjured by her frayed mind, mocking the futility of her plight.

J ess leaned heavily against the wall, each breath a sharp, jagged thing tearing through her. The key in her hand, once a symbol of fleeting hope, now weighed her down with its utter uselessness. Memories surfaced, unbidden—Dee and Josh once mused about a padlocked door in the basement, discussing potential escapes. Their voices, now echoes of a past not so distant, spurred her resolve.

"The basement," she rasped, her voice a broken whisper, clinging to the notion of another exit. Pain flared across her ribs as she pushed off the wall, the moonlight through the barred windows throwing sinister shadows across her path. She took a step, then another, her movements cautious, deliberate.

Above her, a faint creak sounded. Jess stilled, heart slamming against her chest. Was it the house settling, or something more sinister? Memories of Mimi's fall, the horrific crunch of her body, the blood seeping into the floorboards... she had to be dead.

But doubt gnawed at her, insidious and persistent. Jess had witnessed too much, seen the impossible become possible.

"She's dead," Jess forced the words out, her voice a mantra against the darkness as she moved towards the basement door. "She has to be."

Another creak, unmistakably closer, halted her. The sound was too deliberate, too ominous. Rationality warred with raw, visceral fear. The old house might groan and complain, but this was different, this was calculated.

The basement stairs loomed before her, a gaping maw in the moonlit gloom. A cold draft rose from below, carrying the musty scent of decay and forgotten things. Jess's hand flew to her side, fingers pressing into the bruise that painted her skin with shades of pain.

"You can do this," she murmured to the darkness, a feeble attempt to steel her nerves. "Just find the door."

The wood above groaned again, a clear and definite sound that sliced through the silence. Whether real or conjured by her frayed senses, it spurred her into motion. Jess descended, the staircase creaking under her weight, each step a protest of age and neglect.

Drip, drip, drip—the sound of water hitting stone punctuated the heavy air, a macabre metronome marking her descent into the bowels of the mansion. Shadows danced on the damp walls, thrown by moonlight that flickered through a dirt-smudged window. Each beam felt like a spotlight on her creeping form, a silent accusation in the vast darkness of the basement.

Jess's foot hesitated mid-step, landing softly on something unsettlingly pliable, not the familiar, albeit uncomfortable, rotted wood and debris she'd navigated before. As the cloud cover thinned, a shaft of moonlight pierced through the high basement window, revealing a ghastly sight.

Josh's face, his expression fixed in a mask of terror, looked up at her from the floor. Where his eyes should have been, only dark, blood-crusted sockets remained, gaping back at her. His jaw was unnaturally agape, as if caught mid-scream when death seized him.

A surge of nausea overwhelmed Jess. She recoiled, her back slamming against the cold, damp wall, and retched. The acidic taste of bile scorched her throat, a stark contrast to the cold horror that enveloped her.

"I'm sorry," she whispered with a rough voice into the suffocating silence, her voice breaking with grief. Josh couldn't hear her—another friend lost, another soul claimed by this cruel house.

Gathering a shaky breath, Jess steadied herself against the wall. With great caution, she maneuvered around Josh's body, her movements hesitant, probing the ground before fully shifting her weight. Ahead, the silhouette of the padlocked door emerged from the darkness, its promise of escape now tinged with dread.

The key, cold and heavy against her clammy skin, almost slipped from her trembling fingers as she brought it to the lock. "Please," she murmured, her breath a mist in the chilly air. The key resisted at first, stubborn and unyielding. Then, with a gut-wrenching scrape that sent a shiver through the basement, it turned.

A loud click shattered the haunting silence, bouncing off the stone walls, ominous and final. Jess's heart raced, her chest tight with a mix of hope and fear, as she pushed against the door, inching towards freedom—or further into her nightmare.

The door creaked on rusted hinges as Jess forced it open, the moonlight spilling into a chamber starkly at odds with the ruin above. The room was unnervingly pristine, each corner arranged with a disturbing level of care.

Directly ahead, the unsettling sight of a figure seated in an antique rocking chair made Jess's blood run cold. The figure sat rigidly, dressed in a bygone era's finery, a cracked porcelain mask where the face should have been, its painted smile frozen in a grotesque grin. Moonlight glinted off the mask's shattered edges, throwing sinister patterns across the room.

Jess stifled a gasp, her hand clamped over her mouth.

To her left, a ghastly tableau held court on a small table shrouded in decayed lace: a tea party presided over by a child-sized corpse, its skin shriveled to the bone, clasping a teacup brimming with dark, congealed liquid. The vacant sockets of the corpse seemed to watch her, a silent accusation in their depthless stare.

The air was thick with the stench of formaldehyde, cutting through the mustiness with its sharp chemical bite. Each body was positioned with eerie precision, as if part of a grotesque museum display designed to mock the living.

Dragging her trembling legs forward, Jess moved deeper into the room. The scenes grew increasingly macabre. A "father" figure stood over a smaller, "child" figure, its hand raised as if frozen mid-strike, the child's mask split as though flinching from the blow.

A grotesque "family" dinner scene unfolded at a long table. The figures were dressed in rotting finery, forever posed in the act of dining on plates heaped with decomposing remains. At the table's head, the "mother" wore a mask elaborately painted but webbed with cracks, overseeing the macabre feast with a counterfeit serenity.

The dead eyes of these preserved corpses haunted Jess, seeming to track her movements through the room, whispering of unspeakable acts sealed within this crypt.

In a far corner, a "couple" was locked in an eternal waltz, their bodies grotesquely entangled. The female's mask depicted peaceful repose, while the male's showed a grimace of pain, their clothing meticulously preserved against the ravages of time.

This chilling choreography displayed a madness that was methodical, obsessive. Each setup meticulously crafted, years of madness distilled into frozen moments of horror.

As clouds shifted outside, altering the moonlight's path, the masks appeared to twitch, their expressions morphing subtly under the capricious light. The atmosphere was heavy with the imprint of countless deaths, each one a silent testament to Mimi's dark descent into madness, preserved here in her underground sanctuary of sorrow.

Jess's gaze snagged on movement in the periphery, a horror unveiled by the pale moonlight. There, slumped against the wall as if carelessly set aside, was Micah, her lifeless form cradling a shattered porcelain doll in her lap. The doll's face was a spiderweb of cracks, mirroring the grotesque distortion of Micah's own visage.

Her knees nearly buckled under the weight of the sight. Jess clung to a nearby chair, its ancient timbers groaning beneath her grasp. Micah's head was grotesquely twisted, her features a mangled tapestry of dried blood and shattered bone, recounting the brutality of her last moments in dark, gruesome stains.

"No," Jess murmured, a bitter taste climbing her throat. She recalled Micah's final, frantic pleas, the haunting thud of her body collapsing, the sickening sound of metal crushing bone—and Jess had fled, abandoning her in her final agonizing moments.

A wave of guilt surged, crashing against her with suffocating force. Her fingers curled into the decayed back of the chair, wood splinters piercing her skin, though the sharp pain was nothing compared to the torment of her remorse.

Then, a soft, eerie voice sliced through the thick silence, seeming to emanate from the very walls, echoing eerily off the macabre masks surrounding her. It twisted, warping into something ghastly, a grotesque perversion of childish innocence.

"No, no, no," Jess muttered, her hands pressing against her ears, eyes squeezed shut in a vain attempt to block out the haunting melody. "It's not real. You're not real."

Despite her efforts, the singing seeped through, a toxic whisper that filled her consciousness, overwhelming her senses until the room and its terrors spiraled into a vortex of sound and fear, leaving her gasping for air amidst the stifling darkness.

The melody crescendoed, each note slicing through Jess's consciousness like jagged shards of glass. Her legs faltered, and as she stumbled backward, a wooden chair clattered to the ground. The crash echoed hollowly, overwhelmed by the singing that intensified, enveloping the room in its nightmarish volume.

"Ring around the rosie..." The words, malformed and eerie, reverberated against the walls in a ghastly childlike timbre. Jess's vision wavered, the room's masks seeming to animate under the moon's glow. Their painted grins widened, grotesquely mocking her fear.

Her shoulder brushed against one of the corpses, sending it crashing from its perch. Its porcelain mask hit the ground and burst apart, its fragments scattering like the teeth of some monstrous creature, merging with the melody to orchestrate a chilling cacophony that frayed the edges of her sanity.

"Pockets full of posies..." The voice seemed omnipresent now, closing in from every conceivable direction. Desperation clawed at Jess as she made for the exit, her hands dragging along the cold, unforgiving stone. The room tilted chaotically, the preserved bodies seeming to reach out and snag her with their withered limbs as she fought her way past.

The air thickened, each inhalation a battle through the pervasive stench of decay and the sharp bite of formaldehyde. Her lungs seared with effort, the lullaby burrowing insidiously deeper into her psyche. Around her, the ghastly assembly of masked corpses bore silent witness to her plight, their empty sockets gleaming macabrely in the lunar light.

"Ashes, ashes..." The child's song climaxed in a deranged crescendo. Jess's skull threatened to split open from the pressure. She lunged for the door, her fingertips just brushing the rough wood—freedom mere inches away.

Suddenly, from the shadows, a hand snapped out, seizing her wrist with iron-like force. Pulled sharply through the threshold, the lullaby ceased abruptly, snuffed out as though it had never been. The final, haunting refrain of "we all fall down" dissipated into the silence that followed, leaving a deafening quiet in its wake.

FINAL STRUGGLE

J ess's heart hammered against her bruised ribs as she wrenched her arm free, spinning to confront her assailant. Pain surged through her battered body with each movement, a visceral reminder of the night's brutalities.

Moonlight streamed through the high basement window, casting Mimi's silhouette into sharp relief against the grim backdrop. The porcelain mask shone with a ghostly luster, its shattered visage a mosaic of dark, dancing shadows on the cold stone walls. Dried blood crusted its fractured edges, stark evidence of the violence Jess believed had ended Mimi.

"You're supposed to be dead," Jess rasped, her voice a raw scrape of fear and fatigue. Her eyes scanned the dim cellar desperately, seeking anything to use as a weapon. Her gaze fixed on a wine rack against one wall, bottles layered with dust but intact.

As Mimi's head unnaturally tilted, the mask's painted smile seemed to stretch wider. Her tattered dress, stiff with old blood, rustled with each calculated step she took toward Jess.

Heart pounding, Jess darted toward the wine rack, her hand closing on a bottle's neck. She smashed it against the wall, the bottom breaking off to leave a jagged, glistening edge. Armed with this crude weapon, she faced Mimi, the broken glass catching the moonlight, sharp as a row of teeth.

Her muscles screamed in protest as she charged, the broken bottle held aloft. "Fucking die!" she screamed, her voice tearing through the suffocating silence as she swung at Mimi's masked face.

The glass struck with a horrifying crunch. Porcelain shards erupted outward as the mask shattered, revealing the grotesque, scarred flesh beneath. Twisted scars marred Mimi's face, the skin puckered and warped as if melted.

Mimi reeled backward from the blow but recovered, her laughter echoing high and haunting through the chamber. It shattered the stillness, a cacophony of madness that reverberated off the stone walls, multiplying and swelling until it seemed as if the laughter came from every shadowed corner of the basement.

Mimi lunged with jerky, unnatural movements. Moonlight highlighted the grotesque twists of scars visible through the remnants of her shattered mask.

Her nails, sharp and unyielding, slashed across Jess's forearm, slicing through fabric and skin alike.

"Fuck!" Jess cried out, staggering back as pain flared up her arm. The bottle she'd been clutching slipped from her grasp and crashed to the stone floor, its shards scattering into the shadows. Blood seeped from the deep scratches on her arm, darkening the fabric of her torn sleeve.

Cornered, Jess's back slammed against the cold, damp wall as Mimi advanced relentlessly. The air in the basement grew thick, mingled with the odors of decay and fresh blood. Frantic, Jess's hands found the back of an old wooden chair, its wood rotting and joints weak. Ignoring the splinters piercing her palms, she gripped it tightly.

Mimi's laughter, broken and chilling, filled the basement, reverberating off the stone walls and multiplying, creating a cacophony of eerie echoes that seemed to come from all directions. The part of her face not hidden by the mask contorted into a grotesque semblance of a smile, more a snarl of triumph.

"Stay back!" Jess shouted, brandishing the chair like a makeshift shield. Each movement shot pain through her bruised ribs, the agony sharp and biting with every desperate breath.

Undeterred, Mimi continued her approach, her tattered dress brushing the floor with a sound reminiscent of dry leaves dragged across stone. Jess, driven by terror and desperation, threw the chair. It shattered against Mimi's chest, the impact sending splinters flying.

Not pausing to see the effect, Jess lunged for a stack of old wooden crates, pushing them over. The crates crashed down, their contents spilling and wood splintering in a loud, chaotic heap across the floor.

"Just fucking die!" Jess screamed, her voice hoarse, her words echoing off the walls, momentarily overpowering the sinister laughter of her tormentor.

Mimi, undaunted, stepped over the debris with eerie fluidity, her movements betraying an inhuman grace. Her shadow, cast long and twisted by the moonlight, morphed into something vast and monstrous on the stone floor. She advanced, the remnants of her mask's painted smile catching the dim light, reflecting a malevolent joy as she closed the distance relentlessly.

Jess retreated into the macabre museum of preserved bodies, her heart slamming against her chest. The overwhelming reek of formaldehyde mingled with the sickly-sweet odor of decay, infiltrating her senses as she ducked behind a nightmarish diorama—a "family" grotesquely poised around a dinner table, their skin mummified and taut over brittle bones. Jess's hand clamped over her mouth to stifle her desperate breaths.

"Where are you, little mouse?" Mimi's singsong taunt floated through the basement's stale air. "Don't you want to join my collection?"

Slivers of moonlight spilled through the high window, casting eerie shadows that danced over the displays. The corpses seemed to turn their vacant sockets towards Jess, their silence a grim testament to her potential fate. Droplets of blood from her slashed forearm fell to the stone floor, sounding unnaturally loud in the silent tomb.

"Such pretty skin," Mimi cooed maliciously. "It would look lovely stretched over wire, preserved forever in my gallery."

Footsteps scraped closer, the sound a chilling promise of impending horror. Jess pressed further into the shadows, her back cold against the wall. Over her, the "mother" figure loomed, its mouth eternally agape in a silent scream of horror or supplication.

Suddenly, a blur of white caught Jess's eye. Mimi, moving with nightmarish speed, crashed into the tableau, upending the grim assembly. The table shattered under the assault, sending mummified limbs and fragments of porcelain flying like debris in a storm. The "mother" figure toppled towards Jess, its wired arms extending like the branches of a dead tree.

Rolling to the side, Jess's hand found the limb of a mannequin. The preserved flesh was cold and hard in her grip. With a surge of adrenaline-fueled strength, she swung it hard, striking Mimi across her fractured mask. The porcelain shattered further under the force, causing Mimi to reel back, her usual maniacal laughter morphing into an enraged snarl. The room echoed with the clash of Jess's makeshift weapon against the unhinged assailant, a sound as desperate and dangerous as the struggle itself.

Jess clutched a splintered table leg, its jagged edges a desperate promise of defense. Her muscles burned with exertion as she thrust the makeshift weapon forward, driving it into Mimi's side. The sound of wood piercing fabric and flesh was sickening, a wet, tearing noise that echoed in the cramped space.

Dark blood spread across Mimi's already-stained dress, yet she barely registered pain. Instead, a chilling laughter erupted from her, filling the room as she seized Jess by the throat with a grip that seemed more than human. Moonlight gleamed off the remnants of her porcelain mask, the once delicate smile now a twisted sneer.

"My turn," Mimi hissed, the twisted flesh around her mouth curling into a grotesque imitation of a grin.

The force of Mimi's shove expelled the air from Jess's lungs as she was thrown to the ground. Her head struck the stone floor, sparking a burst of stars across her vision. A metallic taste flooded her mouth, mingled with the sharp tang of panic.

Through the haze of pain, Jess saw the heavy metal table laden with Mimi's macabre trophies nearby. Ignoring the protest of every bruise, the raw scrape of her skin, she summoned her waning strength. Pushing against the chilly stone, she staggered to her feet, her surroundings tilting dangerously.

"Fuck you!" Her voice was a raw, torn sound as she hurled herself at the table. Metal shrieked against the floor, sliding with a grating sound and striking Mimi in mid-lunge. The table pinned her against the wall, the impact issuing a gruesome crunch of bone and flesh.

Mimi's form sagged, the fight draining out of her as her head drooped, the remnants of her mask clinking down to join the debris on the floor. Silence surged back into the basement, filled only by Jess's labored breathing and the steady, sinister drip of blood.

With every ounce of remaining energy, Jess staggered towards the staircase, her legs nearly buckling under her. Blood wept from a cut on her temple, blurring her already unsteady vision. The reek of death hung heavy in the air, a foul specter that clung to her, permeating her clothes and skin as she made her escape from the basement of horrors.

Jess clawed her way up the stairs, her body a map of pain, each step a sharp reminder of her injuries. Blood dripped from the gash on her temple, tracing a chilling path down her neck. The oppressive darkness of the basement reached for her, eager to reclaim its fleeing captive.

A sudden, chilling hiss shattered the suffocating silence.

Without warning, something rough and cold constricted around her throat—an extension cord, its bite searing into her flesh. Jess was jerked backward, her brief glimpse of escape brutally snatched away. She gagged, air cut off, as her hands desperately grappled at the cord.

"Pretty little mouse," Mimi hissed into her ear, her voice no longer melodic but a terrifying, guttural snarl that froze Jess's blood. "Running away so soon?"

The cord tightened mercilessly. Jess's fingers struggled against the implacable grip of the rubber, her skin tearing, blood welling under her frantic nails. Her vision tunneled, edged with encroaching blackness. The stairwell seemed to spin, the macabre tableaus of the preserved corpses blurring into ghastly specters that mocked her with silent, stitched smiles.

Hot, foul breath washed over her neck as Mimi leaned in closer, the jagged edges of her shattered porcelain mask scraping against Jess's skin. Each labored, burning breath Jess took was a battle, fought in the shadows that now seemed to pulse with malicious intent.

The grotesque audience of mummified corpses appeared to watch, their empty eye sockets and grimacing mouths forming a choir of silent mockery, witnessing her struggle.

Desperation surged within Jess as the darkness threatened to engulf her consciousness, her body weakening with the struggle for oxygen. The macabre figures loomed, a gallery of the damned, their presence an eerie testament to Mimi's madness—a madness that now sought to claim Jess as its next artifact.

Each gasping attempt at air seared her lungs, the world tilting into a vortex of pain and panic. The shadows of the basement drew nearer, whispering promises of oblivion, ready to swallow her whole into their eternal, silent maw.

Jess's mind, starved of oxygen, screamed for her to move, to fight back with every shred of her being still clinging to life. In a burst of primal desperation, she slammed her foot against the base of the staircase, the force catching Mimi off balance. They crashed to the ground together, the cord around Jess's neck slackening momentarily. Pain exploded across her body from the impact, reawakening her battered ribs, yet the rush of air into her lungs was intoxicatingly sweet.

Mimi's shriek tore through the stifling air of the basement, a sound teetering on the brink of madness—part fury, part perverse joy. As they struggled, shards of her shattered mask dug cruelly into Jess's skin, mixing blood with the salt of her tears, obscuring her vision further.

Dragging Jess across the cold stone floor, Mimi headed toward the chilling exhibition of preserved bodies. The vacant, mummified figures appeared to watch eagerly, as if anticipating Jess's inclusion in their eternal, silent gathering.

"Hush, little baby, don't say a word..." Mimi crooned, her voice morphing into a ghastly lullaby, bizarrely childish, emanating from behind the jagged remnants of her mask. The melody echoed unnaturally around the room, amplifying in the enclosed space until it seemed as though a chorus of the damned sang with her.

As the basement spun around her, Jess's bloody hands could no longer maintain their grip on the cord. Her arms dropped, heavy and defeated, to her sides. The encroaching shadows of the basement mingled with the darkness clouding her vision, distorting the ghastly smiles of the corpses into grotesque smirks.

As her consciousness waned, the sinister chorus of Mimi's lullaby was the last sound to pierce the fog of her mind. Silence enveloped her like a shroud as the shadows claimed her, pulling her into an abyss where the stitched, grinning faces of the preserved bodies were the last images etched into her fading sight.

DAWN'S GRIM SILENCE

EPILOGUE

Through the fractured facade of her porcelain mask, Mimi surveyed her dominion, her gaze sweeping over the carnage that adorned the concrete beneath her. Blood, vibrant and dark, painted chaotic masterpieces on the floor, intermingling with shards of broken glass and remnants of splintered wood. Her grip tightened possessively around Jess's ankles as she hauled the inert body deeper into the sanctum that whispered of eternal silence, all the while humming a haunting lullaby once sung by her mother.

The basement's atmosphere was dense with the iron tang of fresh blood and the pungent aroma of formaldehyde, a testament to the meticulous preservation pervading the air. Slivers of moonlight seeped through the barred windows, stretching long shadows across her collection, her created family, forever captured in their designated poses—preserved, perfect, perpetually masked.

"We have a new sister," Mimi cooed with a disturbingly childlike delight to the assembled figures around her, their vacant gazes fixed in frozen watchfulness.

Her attention drifted momentarily as she caught the sight of something amiss—a shard of her own broken mask on the gritty floor. The crack, a jagged scar across the once flawless smile of her mask, was a glaring imperfection. She traced the rough edges with a tender touch, a pang of unease fluttering in her chest. Imperfection was unacceptable; mother had always insisted on maintaining appearances, on the facade of pristine normalcy.

With a measured grace, Mimi floated to a secluded corner of her basement, where her reserves lay—a collection of masks, each crafted with an eerie devotion. These were the faces for her ever-expanding family. She selected a pristine white mask adorned with delicate blue flowers encircling the eyes—its previous owner no longer needed it, having made the fatal error of attempting escape.

Moonbeams played through the grime-tainted windows as Mimi approached a tarnished mirror. The glass, marred by the passage of time, reflected her distorted image, the cracks echoing the fractures in her psyche. Carefully, she dislodged the damaged mask, setting it aside with a reverence born of madness. The chill of the new mask against her marred skin felt like a balm, fitting seamlessly, as if reclaiming a part of her lost beneath the painted porcelain.

A giggle, soft and chilling, escaped her as she adjusted the mask, ensuring its symmetry—the embodiment of the perfection her mother had instilled. The giggle ricocheted off the cold basement walls, intertwining with the profound silence of her motionless audience. In the mirror, the fresh mask smiled back at her, a smile unscathed by the brutality of her existence. Order restored, her world was once again immaculate—a portrait of deranged perfection.

Through the fragmented visage of her freshly donned mask, Mimi dragged Jess's lifeless form across the basement's cold, concrete floor. Each pull left a macabre trail of crimson, like paint strokes on the grim canvas of her sanctuary. The extension cord looped around Jess's neck swayed with a grotesque grace, a morbid adornment that seemed to whisper approval to Mimi's fractured psyche.

The chaise lounge in the corner beckoned—a faded relic upholstered in once-lush velvet, now marred by time and tears, yet perfect for her newest sister. Mimi's movements were methodically tender as she manipulated Jess's limbs into a deliberate repose; one arm languidly draped over the chaise's side, fingers poised in an eternal, elegant gesture of reaching. The other arm she laid across Jess's chest, the hand open, inviting the world or perhaps beseeching some unseen mercy.

"Like sleeping beauty," Mimi murmured as she brushed clotted strands of hair from Jess's face. Her voice carried the lilting cadence of a lullaby, reminiscent of those her mother hummed during nights shadowed by illness. "Hush little baby, don't say a word..." Her song fractured against the stark concrete, shards of melody bouncing off the walls in a dissonant echo.

She adjusted Jess's head with meticulous care to ensure the angle was just so—artfully tilted to suggest a natural rest rather than a violent end. Mother had always emphasized realism in their family portraits. "They should capture real moments," her mother's words echoed in her mind. Mimi's giggle cut through the silence, its sound breaking into something jagged and chilling.

Stepping back, she surveyed her work. Jess's vacant gaze met the ceiling, her eyes frozen wide with the remnants of terror. Moonlight sluiced through the barred windows above, casting stark shadows that contoured the bruises encircling her neck, lending them a perverse beauty, almost picturesque in their stark brutality.

Mimi spun, her ragged dress catching the air, shadows swirling around her in a macabre dance. The silent watchers—her family encased in their eternal masks—seemed to revel in her delight, their painted smiles stretching wider in the dim light. She halted abruptly, head tilting, drawn by a faint creak from above.

The sound, real or imagined, pricked at the edges of her elation. Was it the house settling, or had her sanctuary been breached? Mimi's eyes narrowed behind her mask, a shiver of anticipation—or was it apprehension?—trickling through her.

Through the eyeholes of her mask, Mimi tilted her head, a creak from above piercing the stillness, igniting a memory—mother's fingernails gently scratching her scalp during nighttime tales. Another creak sounded, then all fell silent.

A giggle started deep within her, a soft chuckle swelling into wild, echoing laughter that reverberated off the cold basement walls. It harmonized with the rhythmic dripping of blood from Jess's now still body.

"The dead live here," Mimi crooned, her voice adopting the playful tone of a child's nursery rhyme. She spun once more, her dress stained with the dark evidence of the night's deeds, swirling around her. "And so do you. Forever and ever and ever."

Her laughter tapered off to fitful chuckles as she took in her work. Moonlight slanted through the barred windows, casting silvery beams over her tableau—the eternal family: mother at her sewing, father buried in his newspaper, brother mid-game, and now Jess, artfully arranged on the chaise in perpetual slumber. Their masks, a frozen choir of gleaming porcelain grins, mirrored her own twisted joy.

Mimi ascended the wooden stairs, each step resonating like a note in the dark symphony playing in her mind. Her laughter trailed behind her, fading into the mansion's deeper, ghostly murmurs, intertwining with the legacy of whispered horrors echoing through its halls.

www.ingramcontent.com/pod-product-compliance
Lightning Source LLC
Chambersburg PA
CBHW071419300726
48976CB00004B/1180